sto DETECTIVE

NO DUST IN THE ATTIC

by Anthony Gilbert

This book is a departure for Anthony Gilbert in that it deals with the English underworld. Differences from the American counterpart are marked, but even so, in England or America, murder is still the final answer to the problem of the guy, or doll, who knows too much.

The ubiquitous Arthur Crook stumbles onto a new client in a London railway station, and later saves her, unwittingly, from sudden death on a train. But even his uncanny perceptions do not prepare Crook for the full truth. Janice Grey has guilty knowledge of a gang of jewel thieves and is fleeing her criminal husband. Two murders, traceable to the gang, already have been committed. The discovery of a third dead body hurled from the train implicates the girl through a pair of railway tickets found in the dead man's hat.

The police want to find and protect the girl from the gangster menace, but before they can do so she flees again—into the hands of her enemies. At this point Crook finds himself, for once, on the side of the police. He fears for the life of the missing girl; equally for her ardent suitor, Frank James, who has been framed for murder number four: the violent death of a gangster's moll.

In an eerie chase, the brash cockney lawyer nearly becomes a corpse himself but eventually winds up on his feet, a voluble witness to the operation of justice and the pursuit of love.

No Dust in the Attic

Recent Books by ANTHONY GILBERT

A Case for Mr. Crook
Black Death
Death Won't Wait
A Question of Murder
And Death Came Too
Riddle of a Lady
Death Against the Clock
Prelude to Murder
Out for the Kill
After the Verdict
Uncertain Death
No Dust in the Attic

NO DUST *in the* ATTIC

Anthony Gilbert

RANDOM HOUSE
New York

FIRST PUBLICATION IN THE UNITED STATES 1963

Manufactured in the United States of America
by Vail-Ballou Press, Inc., Binghamton, N.Y.

Library of Congress catalog card number: 63-9828

To Helen

With Love

No Dust in the Attic

One

In the quiet room a shot rang out. It was followed by the sound of a crashing fall, a closing door and the graduated noise of feet running down a staircase.

The girl standing by the ironing board crossed the room and quickly switched off the radio. After nearly twelve months she couldn't hear the sound of a shot, even in a play like this one, without recalling the man shot down in process of a jewel robbery and left to die. The police were still looking for the gang. She shivered, wondering if there was any place on earth where you could escape from yourself.

Then she went back to the ironing board. The cotton dress rose up in crisp smooth folds under her neat hands; she put it on a hanger, spread a blue scarf in its place. She worked quickly and with great care. When you lived in one room you had to be tidy; she'd seen enough confusion during the months of her married life with Pat to last forever. It was the insecurity of that time that returned to her most often, the sensation of coming downstairs in the dark and finding a tread missing from the staircase. By the time she was twenty-one she had learned to hesitate before lifting a telephone receiver, to peer from the shelter of a window curtain before opening a door, to stiffen at the sound of feet coming up behind her on the escalator, even shrink from a casual contact in a crowd.

But all that, she reminded herself feverishly, belonged to

the past. It was absurd to allow a radio melodrama to uncover so much fear. Pat had stopped looking for her, if indeed he'd ever started, and she had recovered some sort of balance, reshaped her existence, known what it was to find pleasure in small things. For almost twelve months she had been living at Mrs. English's boarding establishment in St. Benyons, a neat little market town a hundred miles from London, as pretty as a postcard—you couldn't imagine handsome, dashing, unscrupulous Pat here. She had a job, nothing very special, receptionist to the biggest hairdresser in the place, but the pay was good and the work pleasant and she had this room and sixty pounds saved. She had acquaintances rather than friends, because people are naturally curious, they want to know where you came from and what you did before that; any hint of mystery arouses them, they dig and dig like little terriers. She wasn't unhappy, the peace was a blessing in itself; she was twenty-two years old, small and dark, with hair like a shining black cap, except at the front where it broke into an irrepressible curl. The gray eyes under the feather-light brows were calm again, the mouth faintly smiled. A damask rose Pat had called her when they first met, she nineteen and burning for new experience, he ten years her senior and already with more experience to his name than she could have credited.

It had been a day of immense and protracted heat; in their window box the petunias drooped their pink and purple bells, though the little button daisies around the fringe raised bright, confident faces to the evening light. Always water flowers when the sun's off them, her father used to say in those early years that had seemed so monotonous and to which she looked back now with a sort of surprised joy. Oh well, he and the home had gone with the early years; then for a time she'd had Pat, now she had herself. She filled a kettle in the cupboard called the kitchenette—Mrs. English advertised no midday meals except at week ends—and crossed to the window, throwing up the sash to let the scarcely moving air come into the room. Now she could see clearly into the companion room of the adjacent house—they were all flatlets and apartment houses around here—where a man was writing at a desk. As though her raising of the sash had disturbed him, he lifted his head and met her wide gray gaze.

She stood, immobilized, the kettle leaking a gentle stream over her unnoticing foot. How long had he been in that room, spying on her, plotting against her? Could it be chance, or hasn't even coincidence an arm that long? And what was his next step to be? Returning to her senses, she straightened the kettle and attended to the plants. Then she closed the window, drew the pale linen curtain, all with an air of composure as if she hadn't even seen that face, let alone recognized it. She hadn't started or betrayed herself in any way, she was certain of that; though she had been frozen rigid with shock. From the top of the wardrobe she took a blue fiber suitcase, into which she folded the contents of the three dressing-table drawers and the hooks in the painted hanging cupboard. The last thing she folded was the dress she had just ironed. Her possessions nowadays were very few; linen, cutlery, china such as it was, all belonged to Mrs. English and would be inherited by the room's new tenants. Rooms never stayed empty long at Heather House; sometimes the outgoing tenant met the new one on the stairs, carrying the inevitable suitcase and raincoat.

From her purse Jan took the key of her room and left it on the table. Her rent had been paid in advance for the week to come. She left the light burning, the rented radio playing low. It had gone into some kind of comedy show, but it didn't matter; she didn't even hear it. That and the light would be her alibi; so long as they stayed on, it would be natural to suppose she was still within. On the landing no one stirred. It was Friday night; most of the girls would be washing their hair in preparation for the week end; the young men would probably be at The Barley-Mow playing darts or on the river. The only stable tenants were the handful of elderly people who apparently regarded Heather House as home, and they would be in their rooms, also listening to the radio, or else watching television or even napping. No need to worry about them. As for Mrs. English, there was no fear of meeting her on the way out; you couldn't detach her from her television set after 7:00 P.M. The faintest of electric bulbs outlined the furniture on the landing, the shadowy stairs, as she came down, gentle and intent as a cat. Tiptoe through the hall—Pat used to sing that song "Tiptoe Through the Tulips," there was no escaping him tonight—open the door, slip through like a shadow, and down the eight steps to the street. But no matter how noiselessly you came, even though you actually held your breath, you couldn't escape Miss Malpas on the ground floor. Miss Malpas sat at her window from dawn to dusk; she noted everyone who passed, everyone who called; she put down the numbers of cars that came back late at night and woke up the tenants. One of these days, she used to prophesy darkly, I may be able to help the police.

"Who wants to?" Frank James would tease her. And she would put on her holier-than-thou look for the young boarder and say it was every citizen's duty.

"I'm like the Scots gardener who was never special struck on duty," Frank said.

Tonight she heard the door close, the quick light feet going down the steps. She drew back close behind her curtains, parting them an inch or two. A girl carrying a suitcase. Well, we all know what that means. Shooting the moon it was called when she was young. Stealing out like a thief—and what more was she? Honest people don't creep away in that furtive fashion. She'd had her doubts about the girl from the start, so pretty, so aloof. People without anything to hide don't mind talking, declared Miss Malpas. But her sugary invitations to come in for a cup of coffee had never been accepted. Miss Hoity-Toity she called her, and decided she'd probably been in trouble. She tried to sound out Mrs. English, but no soap there, as Frank James would say. She watched the girl walk up the street and turn into the mouth of Freeman's Alley. That confirmed all her suspicions. The alley led directly to the station.

"Getting out," Miss Malpas confided to her bird. Having Percy was her substitute for a husband, and he paid her about as much attention as a husband would have done. Miss Malpas considered running down for a word with the landlady, but decided against it. The woman had been quite unpleasant when Miss Malpas had complained very reasonably about Mr. Lander practicing his flute—it wasn't even as though he was very good. The spinster believed in the Biblical theory of repaying fourfold, and that cut both ways. Anyway, she decided, it was too late to catch the girl. No one else knew she had gone.

Freeman's Alley was empty as Jan slipped into it, noiseless as a swimmer sliding under the waves. Not even a cat to be seen. At the far end shone a faint mist where the light from the economical street lamp colored the evening air; it gave a fairytale effect that seemed oddly out of place here. Halfway up the alley a thoughtful local Council had placed a telephone box, and luckily at this hour it was unoccupied.

Nora, Janice thought. Her friend, Nora Penge, with a cool prescience, had said, "If ever you're up against it, there'll always be a bed in my place, even if it's in the cellar." A cellar would be a very good place of refuge just now, Jan decided, setting down her case and dialing for the operator. Nora knew that her friend's marriage had come unstuck, though she was miles from the truth. You couldn't ask your best friend to become accessory after the fact to murder. Though after a first meeting with Pat, Nora had said, "Didn't your mother ever tell you the story of Little Red Riding Hood and the wolf?" She knew there are some things that are too good to be true and Pat Wylie was one of them.

"No reply," said the operator cheerfully.

"Oh, please," Jan begged. This was the last straw. "Do try again. She may be in her bath."

"One of these days they'll start fitting telephone extensions in the bathroom along with the TV," prophesied the girl darkly. But she was a good-natured creature and she tried again, with the result that after about a minute Jan heard the welcome words, "Here's your number."

"Nora?" she called eagerly. "This is Jan. I . . ."

"Wrong number," said a disgruntled voice.

"Oh, but it can't be. I want to speak to Mrs. Penge."

"She's not here. Leased the flat to me for three months. No, I don't know where she is." The receiver was slammed down again. Another temple gone, thought Jan. She drooped against the glass door. What now? She wasn't actually surprised that Nora hadn't told her she was going away; she might never have learned to write for all the use she made of her knowledge. What's the telephone for? Nora would ask. Still, it wasn't possible to go back, the only thing to do was travel to London as she had planned, and look around for a room when she got there. Paddington was circled with boarding houses and flatlets, there must be some corner where she could fit.

A hand tapped on the glass, a polite reminder that the box wasn't there solely for her convenience. She stooped to recover her case, then turned, a smile on her lips. But it vanished like a genie an instant later, because the face peering through the glass was the face she'd seen through a window half an hour earlier, the face of her husband, Pat Wylie, whom she had hoped she need never see again.

His hand came out, pulling the door wide. "Running away again, darling? It's becoming quite a thing with you. Did you think I wouldn't catch up with you when I was good and ready?"

"What do you want?" she whispered. "Why did you come?"

"When a man sees his wife beetle off with a suitcase it's reasonable to suppose she's making a bolt of it, and next time Fate mightn't be kind enough to let me know your whereabouts. You've given us quite a dance. Who put you up to it? Buying a ticket for Wales, I mean, and leaving it where I couldn't help seeing it, and then going somewhere quite different the day before?"

"It was a book by John Buchan," she said, and he laughed.

"You haven't changed," he said. "You were always the original little girl, sugar and spice and all that's nice."

He hadn't changed: same mobile mouth with the smile that hardly ever reached the eyes; warm, caressing voice; eyes black and bright and shallow as a bird's, hard as bits of coal. Under the trim mustache the white teeth shone.

"Who was that you were telephoning?" he went on. "Oh well, I daresay she can put up two as well as one, when it's a husband and wife." His hand closed around her case. Jan shook her head.

"It's no good, Pat. We've nothing to say to each other now." She wrenched her arm free.

"Speak for yourself, sweetie." The charm oozed out like toothpaste from a tube. "I've been saving it up for nearly a year. Where did you get to? You're like the partridge that can sink into its surroundings and become invisible till it's flushed by a clumsy foot." He looked down with a brief, apologetic laugh at his own beautifully shod slender feet.

She struggled for possession of her case. "No. Give it to me. I can manage. It's not heavy."

He weighed it critically. "With all my worldly goods I thee endow. Not a large endowment, would you say? Now, don't let's start anything here. I'm coming with you and that's that. So—lead on, Macduff."

She fought him silently, with about as much chance of success as a canary battling with a hawk.

"I've nowhere to go," she assured him. "She's gone away, let her flat."

"Then we'll share a bench on the Embankment," he soothed her, "keep each other warm."

Sudden anger flared in her voice. "Leave it alone," she cried. "It's mine." And, as though that was a prearranged signal, feet sounded nearby, and a policeman loomed up in the alley.

"What's going on here? This man bothering you, miss?"

It wouldn't be the first case of telephone pests annoying young women.

Pat stepped back. "Go on, sweetie," he said. "This is where we came in. It was through a policeman we got acquainted."

Panic froze her tongue. It was her chance, but she couldn't take it. The truth was too fantastic. "It's just—I can carry my own case," she muttered, sounding like a sulky little girl.

"You can see what an independent wife I have." Pat smiled. "Now, come along, darling, you've had your fun. We're going home."

Fear came into the little box, making the trio into a quartet. She'd been a fool all these months, supposing she would ever get away.

"Is that true?" the policeman demanded a bit huffily. No one likes being made to look a fool.

"He doesn't believe us," said Pat. "It's as true as God made little apples. You'll find the record at Somerset House."

The constable scowled and moved on. Never interfere between married folk, he'd been warned, not without you're called in special. And even his superior, a tetchy fellow called Bones, didn't blame him for not guessing this was going to blossom into a case of murder.

At the station Pat, still carrying the case, moved toward the ticket office. Two singles to London, he said in his brisk, pleasant voice; then stepped aside so that later, when the inquiries started, the clerk admitted he didn't think he could identify the gentleman. Sitting at the receipt of custom, as it were, passengers became so many faces, nonhuman types really, just hands slamming down silver or notes, voices naming destinations. If you started trying to memorize faces . . . But he remembered the young lady better. Yes, he said later, she was quite young, slim and, he thought, dark. She wasn't wearing a hat; and she had given him such a look. What on earth did he mean by that? Well, just a look, not furious or scornful or impatient, as passengers so often were, but something that haunted you—beseeching was what came into his mind. Mind you, he hadn't thought about her for long. When you lost three hens in a week and no one could put a name to the disease that had carried them off and it could mean losing all the rest, you hadn't much time to bother about even unusual fares. He supposed, perhaps, he'd remembered her particularly because of the way the chap had backed off saying, "You're the banker, my dear," and laughed—but not as though it was really funny. Jan could have told them something about that laugh. Once it had put the sun in her sky, and she wondered how many other spurious suns had dawned for how many unsuspecting people during the year of their separation.

"We've time for a cup of tea before the London train,"

Pat offered, taking the tickets from her unresisting fingers. He'd always had that effect on her, the rabbit charmed by the ferret, even when it knows the ferret's up to no good. "Always supposing the refreshment room's open."

Astoundingly it was. St. Benyons was a rural junction, with lines splaying in all directions. Plenty of passengers found themselves with anything up to an hour to spare before their connection came through, so a benevolent British Railways laid on a special late service for their benefit. Pat dropped the suitcase beside a small table and sat down. Meekly Jan walked up to the counter at the same time as a large, cheerful, rotund figure, wearing the brightest of brown suitings, bounced over to the further end where there were bottles and glasses instead of cups and urns.

The not-quite-young lady behind the counter moved down to attend to him.

"Ladies first." Mr. Crook of London Town beamed.

"First come, first served," corrected the attendant unsmiling.

"I'll be a lady for once," Crook offered, "and not be quite sure what I want."

He grinned at her disgruntled face. The police had been known to observe that it 'ud be a tussle to the death between him and Lucifer when it came to pride, but he didn't expect to be recognized here, or merit special attention if he were. The criminal's hope and the judge's despair, they called him in London; and that was nothing to what some of his fellow lawyers had to say about him. A disgrace to the profession, they said, but Arthur Crook knew his onions and he always contrived to stay just this side of the law.

The woman didn't move. "Anyone can see what the young lady wants is a nice b. and s.," Crook went on. "How about it, sugar?"

"B. and s.?" She looked vague.

"Brandy and soda," amplified Crook with a sigh. You were always being told that country folk were as sharp as cockneys, but you didn't have to believe it.

"Oh no, thank you. Just two cups of tea."

"With or without?" demanded the waitress ungraciously.

The poor girl didn't seem to have all her marbles, or else, amended Crook charitably, she was suffering from shock.

"Why not let the young lady take the sugar bowl with her?" Crook asked. "Anyway, according to my calendar sugar came off the ration a long while ago."

"I don't take sugar," murmured the girl.

"How about the boy friend?" suggested Crook with one of his famous alligator smiles.

"Oh yes." It was almost as though she'd forgotten the chap existed. Something cooking, thought Crook hopefully. As saints can perceive good anywhere, so he could detect the seeds of crime. And matrimony was as fertile a breeding ground as any. It never passed through his mind that they weren't a married couple. Take the word of a bachelor, he used to proclaim. We can't be wrong.

As soon as they had swallowed their tea the couple left the table. The London train went from the further platform, and to reach it they crossed the line by a bridge. As they reached the top of the stairs a rocky-looking female—she wasn't called Capability Jane for nothing—came marching along with a dog on a string. The dog wound itself around Pat's leg and Pat riposted by standing on one of its paws. The dog let out an s.o.s. that could have been heard in Mrs. English's boarding house, and C. J. went off like a giant firework, envenomed stars shooting in all directions.

"Can't you look where you're going," she stormed, "or is it just that you can't walk straight? At this hour of the evening, too. Disgraceful!" She squatted on plump hams and held the dog's paw lovingly, even rubbing it against her red-brick cheek. "One of these little ones," she rumbled.

"I don't know what all the fuss is about," offered Pat in his pleasantest voice. "Even if I'd broken that paw off he'd still have three left, which is one better than you or me."

She looked at him then, a glare of hate under brows like a blackstone cliff. "You'll know me again, won't you?" Pat offered.

And so, in due course, she did.

"These canophiles!" sighed Pat, rejoining Jan on the bridge. "It's a disease really, particularly rampant in the British Isles, though not unknown in the States."

"Cano—?" Her voice was still abstracted, as though her thought was far away.

"Canophiles—dog worshipers. Mind you, I've nothing against dogs so long as they're not kept by people who will spell the word the wrong way round. Then they become a nuisance to the community."

He talked easily and lightly as they descended to the further platform. Not many people were waiting about, and of these no one subsequently remembered the pair. When the train came in Pat moved up near the front.

"Not so far to walk the other end," he explained. It was a long train and a fast one, only two stops before Paddington. They got a compartment to themselves with no difficulty and Pat hoisted the blue case onto the rack. Just as the train was about to draw away from the platform a ginger-colored bombshell came hurtling down the steps and flung himself into one of the rear carriages. The porter, who yelled indignantly, "Stand away there," was rewarded by a great grinning moonface—if you could imagine a mahogany-colored moon—at the carriage window. Then the train drew out.

"Deserves to get hisself killed," was the man's morose comment. But, life being what it is, it wasn't Crook who was going to hand in his dinner pail before the train reached London.

Two

In their carriage Pat lit a cigarette, said cordially, "I seem to remember you don't, do you?" and threw the match on the floor. He had picked up an evening paper at the station and this he now shook out. Jan sat opposite him, hands folded, as helpless as a leaf caught in a wind. In her mind she made plans for evading him when they got to London, but these disintegrated like the curl of ash from his cigarette as soon as she began to imagine them in action. Once or twice a foot passed the carriage window. She wondered what would happen if she made an appeal to a fellow traveler. But she knew. Pat would explain, "I'm taking my wife home—from a hospital? A prison? An asylum?" She had lived with him for less than two years, but she knew that if it came to an open conflict, with spectators, all the sympathy would be his. It flowed his way as water runs downhill. Even she at that first meeting . . .

"Penny for them?" said Pat unexpectedly.

"I was thinking how right Mrs. English was—she was my landlady—when she said that the most important developments in life may depend on trifles so insignificant in themselves . . ."

"It's the little things that matter, don't you see? There's a song about that, or was it before your time?"

"If I'd dialed the right number that first day," she went on absorbed in recollection, "if I'd had enough coppers for a second call, I shouldn't even have noticed you come sliding into the Pikle, we'd never have spoken . . ."

"And you'd never have been Mrs. Pat Wylie. Why were you, by the way?"

She said simply, "I thought it was love. I thought you felt the same."

She was remembering the occasion as clearly as if it had happened last week. Nora Penge had had an operation and was in hospital, and there had been grounds for anxiety. Jan wanted news and during her lunch hour she hung about waiting for an empty phone box. When at last she secured one—there's always a queue in London at midday with men waiting to put something on the three o'clock—in her haste and apprehension she reversed two of the digits. When she found out her mistake the operator wouldn't put her through to the hospital till she put three more coppers into the box.

"But I haven't got any more coppers," she pleaded.

"Be a devil and risk sixpence," the girl advised.

"I haven't got anything but a florin."

"Then you'll have to get change, won't you?"

"Once I leave this box I'll never get another. You know how it is this time of day."

"You should have thought of that before you dialed the wrong number," said the girl pertly.

Jan pushed open the door in despair and at that instant a man came quickly between two tall buildings and entered the Pikle. She didn't pause to consider, but called out, "Oh, please. Please stop."

And he swerved sharply and it was Pat. Nothing could have been more fortuitous.

He smiled, that famous smile that was to be her undoing. "In trouble?"

"I need three pennies and I've only got a florin. It's terribly urgent."

"It must be." He fished in his pocket.

"I'm sorry if I startled you," she apologized.

"Frightened me out of my wits," he assured her.

"Why? Did you think I was the police?" She said it out

of pure mischief and she was a bit surprised at his quick reaction.

"Why do you say that?"

"It's like a film," she murmured.

"With me cast for the villain?" He found three coppers among the coins in his palm and held them out to her. "One of these days some enterprising producer will reverse the situation, and it'll be shown that the interloper, me—he put his hand over his heart and bowed extravagantly—is the actual victim, and the innocent young woman only wants the money to contact her fellow criminal. Or possibly," he added, "to send a poison-pen message over the ether or implement a blackmail demand."

"Are you on the stage?" she asked curiously.

"Not more than the next man. Sometime," he added politely, "when we're neither of us so much engaged, we must have a get-together and exchange our life stories."

She felt the color come quickly into her cheeks as he laughed and moved away. She got the hospital all right this time and it was good news, not to worry, Nora was doing well and could have visitors at the week end. She came out smiling and it seemed the oddest of coincidences that there should be a policeman waiting in the Pikle, who stopped her to ask if she'd seen anyone hurrying through.

"Well, I've been telephoning, I had my back to the street," she pointed out, "but if there had been anyone I might have noticed."

When she emerged into the High Street Pat surfaced again.

"So you're all right," he said, a bit superfluously, she thought.

"Why shouldn't I be?"

"I was afraid I might have made things a bit difficult for you. That bobby—he asked me if I'd seen anyone, and I said only a girl in a telephone box. Then I saw him stop you, and I was afraid I'd put him on the trail."

"He wanted to know if I'd seen anyone skulking through the alley."

"He asked me that, too. It never occurred to me he'd bother you."

"Oh, he didn't bother me. And I hadn't anyway—seen anyone, I mean. Why did he want to know?"

He looked penitent. "I never thought of asking him. Well, since all's well—you look as if the sun had just come out and you looked like the beginning of a wet morning not five minutes ago—why not come and have a drink?"

So that's how it had started, and when she read in the paper the next day that there'd been a daring smash-and-grab—20,000 pounds' worth of stuff taken—it never occurred to her to associate Pat with the affair. Though the setting and the time were right, she couldn't have believed that anyone with such a Damoclean sword hanging over his head could look so unconcerned and gay. And at that time she'd never dreamed that quite soon she was going to become Mrs. Pat Wylie, and within three years would be staring at her husband in a second-class railway carriage, racking her poor, demented brain for some way out of the trap.

So much for holy matrimony, she thought.

Crook would have said, "And how!"

She looked up to find her husband's eye upon her. He put his hand in his pocket and drew out a penny that he balanced on his palm.

"Actually, considering the cost of living, I suppose it should be sixpence," he allowed.

"All right," she said. "Why did you wait for me that first day? Wasn't it taking unnecessary risks? I mean, I could hardly have identified you from two minutes in an alley when my mind was on something else."

"No?" Up went the satirical black eyebrows. "Darling, you wound my pride. As a matter of fact, it was touch and go. That fellow at the jeweler's had a head like an eggshell and there was always the chance he'd snuff it. And then a man needs a wife and you were very sweet. Don't think I'd have come to heel if you hadn't bewitched me. It's a pity really you had to find out about me. We were getting along very nicely. Why did you have to come to London that day and see me talking to Harris? When according to my own version I was en route for Wigan and everyone knows you don't go to Wigan from Victoria?"

"I thought as you were going to be away overnight seeing an important new client—heavy insurance for his wife's jewelry, you said, and with so many jewel thieves about you were kept running up and down the country like a monkey up a stick—well, I thought I'd come up and spend the night with Nora."

"Oh yes. Dear Nora. Your sheet anchor. What did you tell her, by the way?"

"It's what she told me. 'You're riding for a fall, Jan,' she said. 'No one could be as wonderful as your Pat.' "

"Of all the something something Heaven may send, Save me, oh save me, from the the candid friend," quoted Pat. He seemed quite unmoved. "And then next day you heard the police were on the track of a tall, heavily built chap with a scarred face, and you did a bit of your famous arithmetic."

"Even then I was prepared to think it was coincidence and I hadn't really seen you at all. After all, it was two platforms away and when I got to the refreshment room, where I thought I'd seen you vanish, well, you had vanished, and I decided I'd made a mistake."

"Every man has his double," her husband agreed.

"I couldn't believe you were involved in a gang of thieves. It didn't seem to add up. And then I had the proof—that you'd been lying to me, I mean."

"Do tell," Pat coaxed.

"I suppose it doesn't matter now. I was putting out your suit for the cleaners . . ."

He sent her a glance of mock horror. "Not that old cod! Wifie finds passionate missive from dazzling blonde—I always thought those chaps deserved all they got, even if it was the business end of a blunt instrument—I'd as soon go around with a hand grenade in my pocket with the pin drawn . . . Anyway, there never was a blonde. I'm not a great chap for the ladies, they're so darn curious and their arithmetic is so original that sometimes they get a sum right without meaning to. . . ."

"No, it wasn't a letter," she acknowledged. "It was your passport, and I opened it to look at the photograph. They're usually such caricatures. And I saw it was your likeness, but someone else's name."

"Actually my name," Pat told her. "My adopted name. Well, why not? Authors do it. Actors do it. Businessmen do it. You don't suppose the names over shop fronts are always the genuine article."

"It's different," she insisted. "You know it's different."

He was musing, still apparently quite untroubled. "A chap I've heard of, though never met—which isn't to say I mightn't one of these days have recourse to his skill—a fellow, believe it or not, called Crook, which seems pretty apposite—holds a theory—so I'm told—that half the chaps who're caught are betrayed by the invisible witness. That is, the one they couldn't guard against, because they didn't know of his existence. The old girl who spends her time looking out of the window . . ."

"Like Miss Malpas."

"Whoever she may be. Well, they're the ones who notice something just a shade out of the straight. Or the woman whose doggie feels the call of nature at 2:00 A.M. when all respectable dogs are in their baskets or on Mummy's bed. There's a classic case of a fellow who had a row with his wife and flung out of the house in the small hours just in time to see another exasperated husband tip his lady wife out of the window. Yes, it's hard." He drew a deep sigh. "Of course you then examined the passport and found that at the time I should have been in Wigan I was actually in Paris."

"In connection with the Cadogan Terrace burglary two days before?"

"Well, you could hardly expect me to tell you that."

"And you could hardly expect me to guess I was married to that sort of man. The caretaker died in hospital, didn't he?"

"He asked for it." Pat's voice was suddenly grim. "If you thought you had anything against me, sweetie, why didn't you go to the police at the time? It was your civic duty. It's in the book of tables and in the Bible—the son shall betray the father to death and the daughter-in-law her mother-in-law—not that you need Holy Writ for that one, I should have thought—but you didn't make a move, except out of my house."

"I was your wife, they couldn't make me speak. And I hadn't actual proof. It still seems impossible, now I'm talking to you again, that you could be one of a gang who go out to—to rob and despoil and murder . . ."

For the first time he seemed angry, shaking his paper as if he wished it were she he was shaking.

"You talk like a child, Jan. For pity's sake, remember you're twenty-two—quite a big girl. No man who isn't a lunatic sets out with murder in mind, or any actual violence, come to that. You might as well say a chap takes out his car with the fixed intention of running down a pedestrian. Of course he doesn't. But if the damn fool gets in his way . . ."

"It might be his crossing," she flared.

"Even pedestrians are expected to show some sense. When the chips fall against you, a wise man shrugs his shoulders and cuts his losses. If he chooses to risk everything, including his life . . ."

"Don't you even feel guilty?" Her voice was full of an honest bewilderment.

"It's just one of those things."

She was silent for a long time; the train whirled them through a tunnel and out into the pale heliotrope evening. She saw ducks on a pond; a swan floating with one wing uplifted, so that it looked like a child's boat that had been capsized.

"How did you find me?" she asked almost listlessly, as though it didn't really matter, and, come to think of it, it didn't. He'd achieved his end and the means were immaterial.

"Another of those invisible-witness turns. You were in London one day a week or two ago; I happened to see you. I noticed where you went and the train you took, and I heard you ask a porter if it stopped at St. Benyons. So I came down on the next train and—well, St. Benyons isn't the world."

"Too bad you hadn't got a car," she gibed. "Then I could just have been the expendable pedestrian."

"You haven't got there yet. I'm the retiring kind, I don't want the limelight."

"It's no use," she said, "I'm not coming back to you. You can't make me. I don't ask for anything."

"Except trouble. If you know what's good for you, you'll do as I say. Then I might be able to save you, even at the eleventh hour."

To her horror she found she was shaking. "Save me?"

"Didn't you ever hear the story of Bluebeard's wife?"

"What's Bluebeard's wife got to do with me?"

"She committed the unforgivable sin, the sin of curiosity. He must have been fond of the wench or he wouldn't have married her in the first place. There are always alternatives. It's murder, tying yourself up to a woman. Sorry, darling, that was purely academic."

The endearment slipped out so easily—if you hadn't been behind the scenes, as she had been for two years, you'd have sworn he was any devoted husband trying to stop his wife making a fool of herself.

"Why did you have to go ferreting among my things?"

"I didn't. It was sheer chance. Why didn't you keep your passport under lock and key? Your spare one, I mean?"

"You may not believe this," said Pat slowly, "but I really did think of you as a wife, not a spy. Then, having found it, you had two reasonable courses open to you. You could have gone to the police and told them your suspicions and asked for protection. And if you weren't hard-boiled enough to do that, you should have kept your mouth shut and gone on as if nothing had happened."

"Knowing you were involved in—murder?"

"The thing you should never have done—only it's a bit late in the day for me to be giving you this advice—was put us all on our guard. Didn't you appreciate, you little fool, it wasn't only me you had to deal with, but the rest, too?"

"But—murder!" She couldn't get away from the notion.

He shrugged impatiently. "A word in the dictionary like any other. And—tell me this—who were you thinking of when you made a bolt for it?"

It had always been the same. He could always get her into a corner, make black seem like white.

"I felt I couldn't stay."

"Because you couldn't endure to associate with criminals? But had it never occurred to you . . . ?"

"Not till then. I knew you worked for a firm of jewel assessors—is that the term? Afterwards, of course, I recognized the link-up, you could give the others the—"

"Wig-wag? Exactly. So you cut the Gordian knot—to save yourself. You mustn't touch pitch and so forth. Don't you see you're not really any better than any of us? Sins of omission are just as blameworthy as the other kind."

She shook her head. "You could always talk the hind leg off a goat."

He smiled. It was something to realize that smile would never deceive her again. "You're the same stubborn little square you always were. All the same, it's true what I said. You were only thinking of yourself. You knew another stupid chap might get in our way and pay for it, didn't you think you had a duty to him?"

"Of course I thought of it. That's why I said in my letter if it ever happened again . . ."

"That's why I had to come and fetch you. It was very coöperative of you to run into my arms. How about Galahad, though?"

"Galahad?"

"Your young man. Oh yes, I saw you together. Does he know you're a married woman, by the way?"

"It's not anything I'd want to boast of, is it? Besides, why should it affect him?"

"Your heel of Achilles again, darling, only thinking of yourself. Perhaps if he knew you had a husband tucked away, that pure heart of his . . ."

"Be quiet," she cried. "Leave him out of it."

"Not altogether indifferent?" he gibed. "Well, he's out of it now, anyway. Would it be indiscreet to ask what your plans are?"

"I meant to go to Nora, but she's away."

"Just as well. She's hardly my type. What happened to Mr. Nora Penge incidentally?"

"He's dead."

Pat drew a hand like a saw across his throat and quirked an inquiring eyebrow.

"Of course not. He was a racing driver."

"*That* Penge! You never said. And when you got there you were going to spill the beans and she was going to say, This time you must inform the police."

"This time?" Realization flashed into her face. "Oh no," she whispered. "Not again."

"Isn't that why you were getting out?"

She shook her head. "I didn't know."

"Don't you ever read the papers?" He took the one from the seat beside him. INJURED MAN DIES yelled the headlines, and underneath were a few lines: "Thomas Routh, the caretaker at the Stanley Square mansion of Sir Everard Bly, who was dangerously injured three days ago when a gang attacked the house, getting away with a haul of £15,000, has died in hospital without recovering consciousness."

She let the paper fall. "I didn't know."

"And yet you're on the run again."

"I saw you through the glass."

"So you packed a toothbrush and a pair of stockings and rushed out to join your pal. What were you going to use for money if she let you down?"

"I have savings," she said quickly.

He laughed again. "Thrift is one of nature's virtues. Even the caterpillar stores up honey for its young. I remember an aunt of mine telling me that once. You should have married someone like Galahad. Now listen, Jan. Your one chance now is to stick with me. Harris would think no more of blotting you out than if you were a smudge on an envelope."

"Why are you saying this to me?"

"You are my wife. I haven't forgotten, if you have."

"You've managed very nicely without me for nearly a year."

"If you cut adrift from me you're done for. I'm telling you the truth."

In a flash she realized that what motivated him was not affection but expediency. He wasn't thinking of her as his wife, but a hostage. She felt suffocated.

"I'm going along the corridor to freshen up," she said, in unsteady tones, grabbing at her bag as if she feared he'd snatch it from her. The train was rollicking along like a racehorse, it almost threw her off her feet. But Pat sounded indifferent again; he had picked up the paper and was glancing through it.

"Take care how you go," he said. "Accidents do happen so easily. I'll keep an eye on your case. There's only one more stop between here and Paddington."

She looked startled; she hadn't even noticed when the train stopped. No one had come near their carriage. Indeed, swaying along the corridor, she realized that this part of the train was almost empty. The compartments on either side of theirs were unoccupied; farther down an elderly workman lolled in a corner looking as if it would take the last trump to wake him. No help there, she thought. She tried to remember the other people on the platform. Was it possible there was someone on the train who was Pat's ally? She imagined herself darting up to some official at Paddington and asking for help. I believe my husband means to murder me. Well, why not? He's already been involved in two murders. Obviously it wasn't likely Harris was going to take a chance like that.

The door marked LAVATORY was bolted and she tried the door leading to the next coach. This opened into a baggage car and a man in a blue uniform looked up sharply. She muttered something inaudible and retreated. She saw that Pat had come into the corridor, was leaning on the open window; he turned his head and waved to her encouragingly. No one living could take him for a criminal at first glance, she thought. It occurred to her to appeal to the guard, but what could one say that didn't sound crazy? Or hurry through into the next coach and leave the train at Cranley Junction. But she wouldn't get away so easily as that, and anyway Pat was in possession of her suitcase and treasured savings. She'd never put them into the post office because in her heart she had always visualized just such an emergency as this, even if she had refused to believe it. Besides, to leave the train she'd have to pass the carriage where they'd been sitting, and he'd come popping out. And if she was right and Pat had an accomplice on board, she might find herself whisked off to—nowhere.

Behind her a door opened, feet went away through the guard's coach, feet whose owner had no reason to shake as she was shaking now. She saw Pat grinning her way and indicating that this was her chance to freshen up, if she'd meant what she said. She slipped into the little compartment and bolted the door.

When he saw his wife disappear Pat returned to their carriage and lightly swung the suitcase down from the rack. Characteristically, it wasn't even locked. He had noticed the contents of her handbag when she paid for the tickets, so, if she had savings, they were presumably in her luggage. It would be a bore if they had been deposited in a post office, though not insuperable. She had a neat, clear hand not too difficult to copy. He found what he was looking for in one of the ruched silk pockets; he riffled through the edges of the notes in their sturdy elastic band. Fifty plus, he decided, slipping them into his pocket while he examined the rest of the case. But there was nothing more there to interest him, no documents, nothing personal at all, just the usual slips and bras and stockings—all things that you could buy at the department stores. He put the case back in the rack. Jan's words about a man going out deliberately to murder rankled. She made life sound so simple, but it wasn't; it was a jungle; jab, gouge and rabbit punch from cradle to grave, and who was she to expect to lie in a silken bed or sit on a velvet cushion sewing a fine seam? She was down in the dirt with the rest of them, and she'd get as smeared as they.

He took a leather wallet out of his pocket and started to count the notes. He'd got to thirty when he heard a step approaching and slipped the wallet and its contents down the side of the seat. When the door slid back he'd got the paper held in front of his face.

"Feeling better, darling?"

The door clashed to. He glanced up. It wasn't Jan, but a tall man in a blue uniform coat and a peaked cap.

"Tickets?" hazarded Pat. "Let me see, where did I put them?"

The man took his cap off. "No hurry," he said.

Pat stared. "What the hell are you doing here? You were to meet us at Paddington."

"And find you'd skipped off at Cranley Junction? Not likely. You should know Harris better than to think he'd take a chance like that."

"Harris knows I've played ball with him. I warned you we were on our way—I suppose you joined the train at Wakebridge?"

"It's a pity you can't always be so bright. Where's the girl?"

"Just gone along the corridor for a minute."

The train roared around a curve. The workman a bit farther down grunted in his sleep. Never heard a thing, he said afterward.

"I asked you, what are you doing here?" Pat repeated.

"I'll give you three guesses, but they better be quick ones. That chap died, you know."

"I'm sorry about that," muttered Pat. "Not intentional."

"You'll be able to tell him so, won't you?"

It was all very quick and tidy; there was no one in the corridor, and the tall man even remembered to take Pat's hat from the rack and dispose of that, too.

Three

The girl stayed in the lavatory as long as she dared, sluicing the faintly brackish water over her wrists, dabbing her forehead. She found powder compact and lipstick and did what she could to improve her appearance, but she couldn't prevent the rouge from standing out against her cheeks' unnatural pallor and her eyes had the bright impersonality of glass. Fate gives us all one chance, they say. She'd had hers when the policeman hove up in the alley, and she'd passed it by. No reason why fate should single her out for a second, though actually that's what everyone expects. Tragedy is the other chap's cup of tea, never your own.

When someone, muttering, twisted the knob for the second time, she reluctantly collected her handbag and unlocked the door. An irate female pushed past her and shot the bolt with quite unnecessary violence. Janice went into the corridor and leaned against the door through which, at Paddington, she and Pat might be leaving the train. The safe world lay beyond the window, an anonymous, insignificant place where people gathered around television sets or threw darts at the local, or sat about making plans for a tomorrow that seemed as safe as tonight. She thought, with a shock of horror, But I shall never feel safe again. It was frightening to realize that at the moment when you felt most secure, most happy, someone somewhere was struggling in a trap as she struggled now. You could never put your finger on a moment when everyone was at peace.

The immensity of that outside world tempted her. Gently she lowered the window. In a few minutes they'd be slowing down for Cranley Junction. Suppose she swung the door open and leaped out the instant the train stopped. There would be a crowd and no matter how empty a train was, those on the platform always fought like bears to get in. Perhaps Pat wouldn't see her alight, she could walk in the opposite direction, there might be a train standing in the bay. She was so much engrossed by these calculations that she didn't hear the footsteps coming softly up behind her. The first thing she knew, an arm was flung around her neck; she'd have screamed then, but the hand covered her mouth. She'd had one arm actually outside the window; the other was pinioned to her side, but she felt desperately for some handhold. Her urgent fingers touched the door handle and slowly the door began to open. She pulled backward. "Pat!" she tried to say. Something hard, like a ring, touched her lips. She felt a roughened edge, and the blood came pricking through. The train poured itself into a tunnel and at the same moment all the lights seemed to go out. She wondered about the guard, but he couldn't be in the baggage car now or he'd have seen what was going on. Thoughts rushed madly through her head. Pat had arranged this, had known it didn't matter what plans she'd made; Nora had played into his hands by being abroad, nobody knew where she was going, she'd left no note. Beside her the door slammed shut.

"Come along," said a voice, that sounded as though it spoke through a velvet mask. "You don't want to do anything foolish. Like throwing yourself out of the train, I mean. You come with me, you're overwrought, I'll give you a sedative."

She felt herself being urged along the corridor and remembered that the compartment nearest the lavatory was one of the single-sided carriages you sometimes get at the end of a coach. If anyone walked past after Cranley Junction and saw it occupied by two people, it wouldn't occur to him to open the door. She fought silently, but now he was lifting her off her feet. In the distance the blackness was turning a dim gray;

in a minute they'd be out of the tunnel. But a minute would be all he needed. Once in the carriage she could be instantly silenced; a drug, a prick of a hypodermic needle, and then at Paddington someone would be waiting, she'd be another missing girl . . .

And then she heard it, a sound more beautiful than any lark, than Caruso and Madame Patti and Madame Melba all rolled into one, though most people wouldn't have agreed with her. Someone was walking through the guard's car, whistling a tune from *Oklahoma* on a note shrill enough to break the sound barrier.

And accompanying those appalling notes was the tramp of feet, left, right, left, right. She thought madly, I could kiss those feet. She really was in what might be described as a state.

Mr. Arthur Crook had left his coach near the rear of the train and come marching purposefully through the corridors looking in all innocence for the bar. It simply didn't occur to him that on a conveyance of this length some sort of liquid refreshment wouldn't be provided. If it is true that a little learning is a dangerous thing, it is equally true that, on occasion, a whole lot of ignorance can save a life.

Trundling along from Coach B to Coach A, beginning to think, dazed and incredulous, that there was no bar after all, he saw a young female apparently trying to cast herself out onto the track. At the same instant the first coach ran out of the tunnel into the dying light. Crook was no sylph, he'd never have made a marathon runner and he'd never in his life done a work-out in a gymnasium, but his brain could move as swiftly as the racquet of a Davis Cup player. It was his brain rather than his size eleven feet that brought him alongside her, one apelike arm wrapped around the moron's shoulders, the other snatching for the doorhandle. Jan, who had felt herself pushed violently against the door, to whose handle her adversary had given one final, vicious twist, knew herself teetering over black space when she felt a grip on her arm that would show itself as an outsize bruise in the morning. A bristly chin rubbed itself against her cheek, an enormous hand slapped her groping hand down, the door slammed shut just as another door opened and a lady emerged coyly from what she always referred to as the smallest room. What she saw horrified her: a creature like an ape in trousers and the reddest head she'd ever beheld, clutching a girl who didn't seem to be putting up any resistance.

"What is going on?" she demanded, and the orang-utang answered her, just as though it was human, after all.

"Got any Mother's Ruin in that hold-all of yours?" he demanded, indicating an enormous, slightly rundown, Italian-type bag that hung from her skinny arm.

"I don't know what you're talking about," she snapped.

"Brandy? Well, smelling salts. No? They did these things better when good Queen Victoria sat on the throne. Wouldn't have caught a lady out then without her vinaigrette. . . . O.K., sugar"—this to the petrified girl he was clutching much too close to his plump person. "Anyway, how about frozen cologne? This young lady's had a shock."

"And not the only one," muttered the old girl. She and her buddy were known in their South Kensington private hotel as Arsenic and Old Lace. This was Arsenic.

Crook actually put out his spare hand as if he'd investigate her treasure trove himself.

"I'll call the guard," Arsenic threatened.

"You do that," agreed Crook amiably. "Guards are like coppers. When you don't want them they hover in clouds, but when there's work to be done they're away on the horizon telling some chap the time." Arsenic gave him her startled Medusa glance, then wordlessly scuttled through the baggage car and back to her companion, to whom she retailed the story.

"For a minute I thought he was—well, trying to take advantage of her. You do hear such dreadful stories about maniacs on trains, but she wasn't even trying to get away."

Old Lace nodded eagerly. "Perfectly obvious. It was a trick to try and get your bag. The girl was in it, of course."

"It did occur to me he meant to push her off the train, if I hadn't prevented it."

"Do you think we should call the guard?" inquired Old

Lace eagerly. Already she had visions of her photograph in the *Kensington Express.*

"Certainly not," said Arsenic. "He'd only try and make out he was saving her life, and then British Railways will probably give him a medal—always very free with our money, I note—and I'm not going to be a party to a fraud of that nature."

In the corridor Crook faced the shivering girl. "Didn't your mother ever tell you about having consideration for others?" he demanded. "If you're tired of it all, what's wrong with a bottle of aspirin? I'm told that usually does the trick, and you can get one at any of the big stations."

She started to shiver again. "There was a man," she whispered.

"I know. I saw him. At St. Benyons. What's he doing letting you wander about by yourself in this state?"

She didn't see Crook as her savior, she saw him as someone who would prove yet another arrow in Pat's quiver. The mention of St. Benyons increased her suspicions. She'd guessed Pat would have an ally on the train, queer to think she'd actually spoken to him. So for the second time that evening she rejected fate's attempts to help her.

"He's my husband," she said confusedly. "At least—that is—I thought . . ."

She wasn't aware of being able to think anything coherently. At the back of her exhausted mind some tiny doubt niggled, some detail she had subconsciously noticed, that ought to mean something, but she couldn't place it.

Giving her the brush-off? Crook wondered. Some girls don't know their luck. If ever I saw a Bluebeard . . . And aloud he said persuasively, "How about me coming along and having a word?"

"Oh no." She knew what he'd say. I found this little lady trying to fall out of the train, you ought to be more careful. And Pat would come up with his story about mental instability, delusions, running off and using another name. They'd toss the ball to and fro over the net until really she would begin to wonder if she was losing her wits. So she passed up this chance, too. Why didn't she trust him? Don't ask me, Crook would have replied. No one knows why dames do things, half the time not even the dames themselves. And, like the constable at St. Benyons, he knew that once you start interfering between man and wife, without an invitation from either side, you're lucky if you reach your own doorstep with even one eye intact.

The train, gradually slowing down, now came to a halt at Cranley Junction, and "Do you mind?" yelled an aggressive voice in Crook's ear. Instinctively he put his hand over it, feeling he hadn't come so near to losing his hearing since the first war forty years before. A hand on the platform snatched at the door and something like a whale came surging in.

"Let 'em off first," Crook offered, as a suitcase bumped him in the rear. He felt like a pretty solid kind of antelope threatened by twin tigresses. The girl, seeing her opportunity, broke away. As he tried to back down the corridor, he found he was stepping on something and, stooping, realized it was the girl's handbag. She was legging it down the corridor like a lady March Hare. "Hey, you've forgotten your purse," he yelled and she stopped in mid-flight. Someone took the purse out of Crook's hand and passed it down to her. She didn't even send him a thank you, just snatched it and slid back a carriage door, where, presumably, Bluebeard was waiting for her.

Only, as it happened, he wasn't.

Crook trundled back to his own carriage, wondering what all that had been in aid of. There was a man, she'd said. He hadn't seen any man, except a ticket collector who'd gone past the window some time ago. Had a row with Hubby perhaps and thought this was a good way of evening things up. Not logical, of course, but you didn't expect logic of the sex. And a good thing, too. They were dangerous enough without that. He grinned as he regained his place, wondering what she'd make of the card he'd contrived to slip into the outer pocket of her bag before he passed it on.

When she got back to her place Jan was surprised to see the seats she and Pat had been occupying were now filled to overflowing with a pair of large female figures, chatting away yakkety, yakkety, yak. Parcels littered most of the carriage. Of Pat there was no sign. She drew a deep breath of thankfulness. Perhaps if she stuck with these two battle-axes she still had a chance.

The battle-axes, who had been regarding her with what-a-liberty expressions on their faces, came abruptly to life.

"Do you mind closing the door, *if* you're coming in?" said Battle-axe No. 1. "There's a draft."

Battle-axe No. 2 made a pointed remark about the emptiness of the train.

"I was sitting here," Janice explained.

No. 1 reared a head like a floral cockatoo.

"I'm sure you were doing no such thing," she declared. "This compartment was unoccupied. Isn't that right, Amy?"

"I mean, I had been sitting here. I was just standing in the passage to—to get some air. That's my case over your head."

She made a move toward it.

"Take care of my hat," said the one called Amy, bluntly. "Can't you wait till we get to London? It won't run away."

But she couldn't. She knew what that would entail. The battle-axes would fuss and fume and block the doorway and give the enemy just the chance he wanted. It was odd, in a sense, that Pat should have vanished. He'd know the plan had failed. It seemed odder still that he'd waited to attack her in the corridor, since he hadn't, it seemed, intended to shove her out of the train when they were cozily together here. And then the missing cog slipped into place. She had torn her lip on a signet ring. But Pat didn't wear a ring. And that meant, didn't it, that the ginger-headed man wasn't in the malarkey with them, after all.

I ought to have stuck with him, she thought. No good

trying to rejoin him now, though. You could be sure Signet Ring was on the lookout. Probably he and Pat were holed up together somewhere. Or had Pat alighted at Cranley Junction, having passed the baton, so to speak, to the next member of the team? So she yanked the case down from the rack and carried it across to the further corner. This was a corridor seat, and as the train drew into Paddington she might somehow try to make a dash for it. Feeling four eyes fixed on her, she snapped the catches and opened the case. She didn't want anything out of it, but she thought it would be comforting to touch that plump wad of notes that she'd never put in a post office account because there was no knowing when you mightn't have to get out and get out fast, as, indeed, she had done. She dug confident fingers into the appropriate pocket, then turned pale. Because it had gone. Hurriedly she clawed through the contents, in case somehow it had got jolted out, but of course it wasn't there. She had no doubt where it was now, in Pat's pocket. He wouldn't be expecting her to have any more use for it.

The voice of the battle-axe called Amy broke into her thoughts.

"I hope there's nothing missing."

She looked up, dazed. It had been quite an evening, she couldn't focus properly.

"You looked as if you'd missed something," Battle-axe Amy explained. "Let me assure you no one has touched that case since we entered the carriage at Cranley Junction."

"Well, of course not," supplemented No. 1. "Silly really, leaving a case unlocked in an empty carriage."

Jan pulled herself together. In a minute they'd suggest calling the guard, and the last thing she wanted to do now was attract any sort of attention. Pat's voice rang mockingly in her ears. "I'm the retiring kind, I don't want the limelight."

"But there's nothing missing," she heard herself say. "I was just making sure I'd got my passport. You know how it is, when you're looking forward to something, you keep wondering if it's going to be all right. . . ."

Amy unbent a little. "Going abroad tonight?"

"Night flight," she improvised. "Paris." She wondered if they had night flights to Paris. Why hadn't she said Rome?

The other two apparently dismissed Janice from their minds and went into a huddle. She caught the name Edwin and something about poisoning being too good for someone. Choking back a cry, because death seemed all around her tonight, she snatched up her case and walked out of the carriage.

Crook, who never hurried himself when he wasn't being paid to do so, caught sight of her near the ticket barrier. She was explaining she hadn't got a ticket; she'd only just managed to scramble aboard the train. The collector asked her where she got on and she said Wakebridge. It didn't surprise Crook particularly that she should be bilking British Railways of about seven bob, but Crook didn't believe her idea was to save her pocket. No, she'd contrived to shed Hubby somewhere, and now she wanted to cover her tracks. Unless he'd simply walked out on her.

Lucky for her, if only she knew, he reflected. It was one of his truisms that handsome is as handsome does and it does a good many people.

So far as he knew he wouldn't be seeing her again, but he'd be the first to admit he wasn't omniscient, and if sparrows don't fall to the ground without some account being taken of it, beautiful young women shouldn't try to take nose dives from moving trains unless it means something.

"I had a hunch," he told Bill Parsons later, "and my hunches are like that advertising chap's suspenders, they never let me down."

Four

At about the time Janice was going into her famous clinch with Arthur Crook, young Mr. Frank James oiled inconspicuously out of The Barley-Mow, where he had been spending the past two hours, an turned toward Heather House. True, it was early, but beer at The Barley-Mow was even less magnetic than the company, and that was saying something. As he approached Mrs. English's house, where he was also a boarder, he saw that a light burned in the room on the second floor occupied by Janice Grey. It was too late to suggest the pictures, but he thought she might make him a cup of coffee—at least it was a pretext to see her. She made good coffee; and she might be persuaded to come out with him tomorrow night. He'd got a couple of tickets for the local repertory theater. His secret ambition was to write plays himself and it was comforting to see the sort of stuff that did get put on. He was thinking long romantic thoughts about Janice as he pulled out his latchkey and came into the hall. Miss Malpas had given up her vigil for the day, but she had ears like little pitchers, and the way she could distinguish between footsteps would have made her a gift to the local constabulary.

From his first meeting with Jan, Frank had known the oddest sensation at the mere sight of her, like seeing a meteor or something that glorified the fairly monotonous pattern of his life. He came bowling up the stairs and played a tune on her door; he knew she must be there because he could hear the radio singing away like a blooming canary, and he could see the light under the door. But she didn't answer and he thought, philosophically, she might be having a bath down the hall, so he stuck his hands in his pockets and hung around. No doubt about it, there was some mystery here. He'd once asked her outright, "Are you bespoke?" because time's valuable and if she was pledged to some other chap you either had to make up your mind to put up with second-best or go out and knock the fellow's block off. But she'd colored up in the most lovely fashion, like a tiger lily or something, and he got the impression some chap had probably led her up the garden path. Still, time's a great healer, and he managed to winkle out of her that she wasn't engaged, and he could see for himself she didn't wear any rings. He knew remarkably little about her, not even in any detail what her job was. She told him she'd been in London at one time and then moved out a bit; she didn't want to go back to the city, couldn't stand alleged traveling facilities, and he saw her point there. If cattle had to travel the way humans did on subways and in buses, the R.S.P.C.A. would have been on the warpath long ago. As he watched the hall, the bathroom light went out and the door opened.

"And good evening to you, Don Juan," said a voice.

"Was that you in there?" demanded Frank.

"Bathing the body beautiful," grinned the other young man.

Frank scowled. "If it was you, where's Jan?"

"Visiting elsewhere, no doubt. Or gone to the pictures. Or . . ."

"She can't be out," Frank demurred. "She's left her wireless on. And the light."

In the hall footsteps shuffled softly; a voice called, "Mr. James—Mr. James, if you're looking for Miss Grey she's gone."

"Oh God, the hellcat," groaned the bathing gentleman, and fled. Frank ran down a few stairs. He had a foreshortened view of the old face tilted up provocatively toward his. He'd never noticed before what an immense proboscis the old girl had. Run twin buses through it, he thought irreverently.

"Gone where, Miss Malpas?"

"It's no use asking me. She did have her luggage with her, though."

"But that doesn't make sense. She's left her wireless and her electric light on."

The big nose snorted. "A deceitful creature. Of course, that's to give the impression she's coming back. Did she leave her rent on the table?"

"How on earth should I know? I don't go breaking into other people's rooms."

"Or a letter? She didn't go down to have a word with Mrs. English, that I do know. Straight out of the door and up the alley and we know what that means."

"What?" asked Frank obtusely.

"The alley leads straight to the railway station."

Frank turned and flung open the door of Jan's room. He marched in, pulling aside the flowered cretonne curtain that did duty for a wardrobe, flinging open the drawers.

"Not even an odd stocking," he commented bitterly. No note, no cash, no nothing. But why, why? And she seemed to like me, he reflected bitterly.

He came back to the stairhead. "What time was this?"

"As it happened I also had my wireless on, so I can tell you precisely. It was just after half-past seven. There's a fast train to London at 8:16."

Mrs. English, disturbed in the middle of a smashing TV thriller, came bustling out of her room. She lived on what she called the garden floor. "What's going on?" she demanded crossly. They'd just taken a body out of the river, fearfully mutilated, and it took half the fun out of the thing if you had to have one ear open for your boarders.

"It's that Miss Grey," croaked Miss Malpas. "She's flown the coop."

"That she hasn't," retorted Mrs. English. "She paid a week in advance only this evening."

"She's gone anyway," insisted Miss Malpas defiantly. "I saw her go with my own eyes."

"Had a telephone call perhaps," suggested Frank easily.

"No one's rung here. The booth's only just outside my room, as you know, and there hasn't been a call since tea."

There wasn't a late postal delivery and there hadn't been a telegram, and Mrs. English insisted that Jan hadn't had any idea of leaving a few hours before.

"She'd have told me if she was going. Well, stands to reason."

"She lived in London once," said Frank slowly.

"Gone off for a week end perhaps." Mrs. English wanted to get back to the telly, though you could be pretty sure she'd never pick up the threads now.

"She'll ring up tonight, I expect," suggested Frank. "Or there'll be a letter on Monday."

"She could have left a message with me," said Miss Malpas. "I'm always at home."

"She's free, white and twenty-one," Frank pointed out.

There didn't seem anything anybody could do about it. It wasn't till next day, when Mrs. English was doing her week-end ordering, that she met Mrs. Jenkins, who had the house next door, and learned that a fellow who'd only been with her two or three days had taken himself off the previous evening, leaving a hurried note on the table to the effect that he'd had to go to London suddenly and would be getting in touch.

They didn't have a Miss Malpas at her house, so it could be presumed he'd had a telephone call summoning him back to headquarters. Sales representative, I daresay, said Mrs. Jenkins. He had signed the visitors' book P. Thompson and given his address as London, W. 9.

"He'll have to come back for his clothes," Mrs. Jenkins added. "Bound to be seeing him again soon. And of course he paid for the week."

The streets around Paddington swarm with boarding and lodging houses, and though Jan drew no luck at the first three, the fourth, run by a Miss Hiscock, had a vacant room.

"It's late," she said, stooping and snatching at the suitcase. She knew all the tricks. Young women turned up with a second-hand valise in which they'd packed half a dozen newspapers, to give an impression of respectability, when really what they wanted was a tent with a board outside proclaiming what they had to offer. Miss Hiscock was always on guard against that sort. Twenty years ago she wouldn't have taken a girl arriving out of the blue at nearly ten o'clock at night, but the present generation were a feckless lot, accustomed to having too much done for them, she thought darkly, and took it for granted they'd only got to knock on any door to get a welcome. But this suitcase was the real McCoy, and the girl was telling a very plausible story. They say the brain works fastest under stress, and Jan was surprised at her own composure as she explained she'd had a telegram summoning her to London for an audition.

"You're on the stage?" said Miss Hiscock, and she said yes, she'd been doing rep in the country—Devonshire, she added, reminding herself to put Devonshire in the visitors' book—but the company had been disbanded and she'd heard of this chance and anyway things were much more hopeful in London, and if nothing came of this—and of course there was no saying she'd get the job—she could get something else. Young actresses had to be pretty versatile, and it was all grist to the mill in a sense. All this came pouring out with a kind of warmth that was very endearing. Not that Miss Hiscock had ever thought of going on the stage, chancy in more senses than one and no provision made for your declining years, but she saw the lure of it, and nowadays there were laws and unions. "I ask a week in advance," she said, and out came the girl's wallet, so that was all right.

"It's a nice room, quiet," she promised, leading the way upstairs.

In fact, of course, it was like forty others, and forty different tenants could pass through it without leaving any trace; but it had four walls and a bed, and Pat and Signet Ring would have their work cut out getting past Miss Hiscock.

"I only do dinner," the landlady was explaining. "Some

don't take breakfast and some don't like tea and they all want it different hours. There's a café on the corner I can recommend. No meals in rooms because of mice, but no objection to a cup of tea." A small kettle, teapot and cup and saucer were provided. She showed Jan the bathroom. "No charge for baths but please leave the place as you'd like to find it. No men in the rooms, no wireless after eleven o'clock, lights out by midnight." She produced the visitors' book and Jan wrote carefully: Jane Graham. Devon.

As soon as Miss Hiscock had gone, Jan locked the door and went over to the window. The view was over roofs and her heart gave a sudden jump at the sight of a policeman looking like a blue doll in the street below. But the next instant she saw a black cat scaling a gutter, and decided that he canceled out the policeman. When she opened her handbag she found a card in it that she'd never seen before. It fell out of the back pocket and was inscribed: Arthur Crook, with addresses in Bloomsbury Street and Earls Court. After a minute she decided he wasn't a private eye, as she had first thought, but a lawyer. For a minute she stood with puckered brows, wondering why the name should seem familiar. Then she remembered Pat mentioning it. And this extraordinary personality, it appeared, was at her service "all round the clock." She thought it probable she'd call on his services before Pat did. She didn't as yet know that Pat would never want anyone's services again, except those of the mortician.

She had found a lodging just in time. Twenty minutes later the heavens opened and the rain came thundering down as if Noah was once more on the rampage. She reflected snugly that she'd packed some tea in her case, and put on the little kettle.

Half an hour later she was dead asleep in a bed as clean and hard as a coffin; she woke to a London patterned with pale gold sunshine, the air delightfully cooled by last night's storm. Between rows of tiles she discovered a flowering tree in bloom, looking like a bride; and a gull, settled on a chimney pot, gave her a preliminary squawk before it took off for the river. She toyed with the notion of telephoning Mrs. English and Lucille, the hairdresser where she'd been employed, and explaining she'd suddenly had to come to town, but she decided to write instead; tomorrow she'd take a bus into the country and post the letters from there. London's a big place, but even so, an outlying postmark seemed to make her situation safer.

She found the café on the corner, where a girl with a head of minute black curls was putting slices of ham into buttered rolls. Two or three of the plastic-covered tables were occupied by early morning workers, but no head turned in her direction as she came in.

"What'll it be?" asked the girl, her flying hands never ceasing their work.

She asked for coffee and a buttered roll.

"And it is butter," the girl assured her. "I don't have any marge on my premises. New here?" she added.

"I've been in the country, doing rep. But I wanted to come to London."

"Funny," said the girl, setting the coffee cup on its plastic saucer. "My husband and me would give anything to get into the country."

"You have to go where the work is. As a matter of fact, my audition's been postponed for a few days, I shall have to get some sort of temporary job."

The girl nodded. Everyone knew aspiring actresses and art students washed dishes or modeled or worked for one of these we-can-help-you organizations. She put the plate of ham rolls on the counter and began slicing a bowl of hard-boiled eggs. "I did hear The Dolls' House wanted someone," she offered. "It's just along the street, morning coffee, lunch and tea, seven days a week. The pay's nothing special, but you get your lunch, though I should think you'd soon tire of macaroni cheese and shepherd's pie."

"Not a waitress?" asked Jan anxiously. Waitresses were on public view and it would be absolutely typical of Pat to come peering through the glass. The girl laughed and shook her head.

"You need experience to be a waitress, it's a skilled job. This'll be backroom-boy stuff."

She turned to serve a newcomer, and Jan carried her coffee and handsomely buttered roll to a small table against the wall. It occurred to her that during the past twenty-four hours she had lost her job, her home and her security, had been the object of a murderous attack in a fast-moving train and, if her luck held, was about to become washer-up in a Bayswater teashop.

So far as she could see, it didn't make any sense at all.

Mrs. Allan at The Dolls' House asked neither for references nor for an insurance card. Girls looking rather like this one bowled in like hoops, worked for a week, two weeks, even a month, then one morning they just weren't there. When Mrs. Allan had been young there was something called a week's notice, but that appeared to be as much of an anachronism as the dodo. This girl looked clean and honest and was prepared to start work at once.

From ten o'clock onward the crowd came for elevenses; as soon as they were gone the early lunchers started and until 2:30 there was no let-up at all. At 2:30 the café was declared closed, and Jan lent a hand putting the room ready for afternoon teas that began at three o'clock. The rush continued till 5:30 when The Dolls' House closed and the staff straightened everything out for tomorrow. It was nearly 6:30 when Jan got back to Miss Hiscock's, thankful to remember there would be an evening meal ready that she wouldn't have to cook. She realized with a shock that she hadn't thought of Pat for more than eight hours.

Even so, meeting Miss Hiscock in the hall, her heart gave a sudden leap in case somehow he'd tracked her down and would be calling again later, but the woman said nothing, just gave a bright, absent smile and disappeared down the basement stairs.

But through she seemed, pro tem at least, to have escaped from him, during the next twenty-four hours he was going to cause a lot of other people a good deal of concern, though as yet they didn't even know his name.

Five

On Saturday morning, before Jan went out to the Corner Café to get her breakfast, a railway cleaner called Raikes started the ball rolling by turning up a wallet that he found stuffed well down the side of a second-class coach in a siding at Paddington Station. The train was due to pull out at eight o'clock and most of the seats had been reserved in advance. When the cleaners were through, an official would come along and affix the tickets, and long before it was due to leave, the crowds would be swarming aboard looking for vacant places. It was a favorite train to the West Country and no one wanted to stand all that distance.

For the moment Raikes was alone in the compartment. He hadn't been working for British Railways very long—he never worked very long for anyone, having a constitutional disability for perseverance—and he was due to go on a week's holiday that afternoon. He thought it most probable that he wouldn't report back for duty. There was nothing in the job for a chap like him, no end product was the way he put it, and he didn't like London. Doubtless he could find himself something in the south coast town where he was spending his holiday, something less taxing in the way of regular hours, clocking in and clocking off—like a ruddy machine, he thought. He glanced cautiously along the corridor. There was no one in sight. The other cleaners were busy in their part of the train, ridding it more or less successfully of the welter of trodden cigarette ends, candy wrappers, apple cores, all the debris that made Raikes think a self-respecting pig was better than the average traveler. The wallet had clearly not just fallen where he found it, it had been pushed out of sight to prevent someone entering the carriage getting a peep. Raikes could understand that all right; what he couldn't understand was any chap not right up the creek forgetting it was there. Unless, of course, it was stolen property. It was a good-class affair, black morocco with small gold initials in one corner: P.W.W. There was no other identification; the contents, apart from the wedge of pound notes that hadn't so much as been inserted into the pockets, consisted of about three pounds in cash, a partially used stamp book and a bit of paper with some figures on it. Presumably X hadn't yet discovered his loss. A wallet containing fifty pounds or a bit more was worth a telephone call. He'd have enough loose change for a taxi or a subway ticket, and possibly he was one of the careless brigade who don't empty their pockets when they go to bed. The proper course was to turn the wallet in, and if it shouldn't be claimed—some hope—perhaps the finder would be allowed to keep it. But he had a vague idea that anything found on nationalized industry property automatically went to the authorities. He compromised by putting the wallet in his pocket, and continuing with his job. If questions were asked before he came off duty he could produce the wallet and no harm done. If no inquiry had been received it seemed likely the wallet was hot. He found a mackintosh and a brief case in other parts of the train—it was staggering what did turn up. Once it had even been a baby, but it was generally supposed that hadn't been left behind by accident. He took the last two objects to the Lost Property Office, and said casually, "Do people ever claim any of these things?"

"Sometimes. But if they don't live in London and it's not worth a lot, they let it go by default. Mind you, I've known women waiting outside the L.P.O. before it opens to pick up a brown paper parcel worth about five bob."

"Brief case might contain state secrets," he offered.
"And so far as we're concerned they'll stay secrets."
No one came lumbering up asking about a wallet by the time he was due to knock off, so he didn't mention it either. On his way home he stripped the wallet and pitched it into a car cemetery on a bombsite that the authorities hadn't thought worth recovering, presumably because they didn't know what to do with the wrecked and rusted chassis, the torn car seats, useless tires and all the flotsam and jetsam that had nothing to do with cars, with which the site was littered.
With a bit of luck it'll stay there till the next war, he told himself.
But he was reckoning without Miranda the cat.

Miranda was one of the twin scourges of a mild and much-persecuted civil servant called Edgar Barrett. Mrs. Barrett was the other. Both possessed the spirit of amazons. Edgar sometimes thought that if there was anything in the theory of reincarnation, souls transmigrating from one form of life to another in an endless process of evolution, Miranda would end up as some miserable fellow's female Caligula. At other times he decided that Emily—Mrs. Edgar Barrett—was the twentieth-century version of a witch, and he was sure he saw Miranda watching him with a calculating eye. One thing he did know and that was that, figuratively speaking, she and Emily were in a blood bond to keep him down among the dead men twenty-four hours out of twenty-four. Even the local toms fought shy of the big feline queen.
On the night after Janice made her spectacular escape from St. Benyons, Miranda was out as usual, planning to give some poor tom hell. Shortly before 10:00 P.M. Emily closed her library book and said briefly, "Where's Pussy?"
"Anything less like Pussy than Miranda I can't imagine," said Edgar, engrossed in a reprint of a Margery Allingham favorite. "I wouldn't bother, Emily. If the nations do start chucking their atom bombs about, Miranda will be one of the survivors."

"There was a piece in the paper this morning about cats being trapped for their fur," Emily told him icily.

"Even a trap would have too much sense to tangle with her," Edgar urged. "She'll come back when she's ready. She's probably weaving a spell in the old car graveyard."

"My Aunt Alice was right," said Emily. "It's a good thing when you're young you can't see what life has in store."

"That's the first sensible thing I've ever known your Aunt Alice to say," exclaimed Edgar incautiously. He knew what Emily meant, of course. As a girl she'd dreamed of herself settling down with someone like Jack Hawkins or Prince Rainier and look what she'd got.

"You'd better go and bring her in," Emily went on. "You know I can't sleep till Pussy's home."

Edgar meekly got his flashlight and went out. He poked it around the garden, and then his neighbor's garden, in a manner so suspicious that a police constable crossed the road to ask him what he thought he was doing. Edgar said he was looking for his wife's cat. He half wished the bobby would run him in; a cell might be uncomfortable, but he'd have it to himself, and he didn't dare confess that he was terrified of going onto the bombsite after dark. He never took any money with him, but these smash-and-grab boys hit first and searched afterward; and there was always the chance that Miranda would launch herself at him like a sputnik, and the thought of those unsheathed claws made him shudder. The policeman, however, seem quite satisfied, so he floundered among the ruins, tearing his trousers and nearly losing a shoe as something as deadly as a ghost hand caught him round the ankle. After some minutes his beam discovered her; she was crouched, snarling softly over something that was probably a rat, but his vivid coward's imagination transformed it into a human hand. It was neither of these, however, but a black leather wallet with the initials P.W.W. on one corner. Needless to say, the wallet was empty. He thought of hailing the bobby and showing it to him, but he was afraid of the retort—What am I supposed to do about that?—and years of being the underdog made him drop the wallet and follow Miranda home. A wife and a cat, when these were Emily and Miranda, were as much as even a hero should be expected to tackle, without the police thrown in. And he had never been a hero!

That was Saturday night.

Mrs. Allan had asked Jan if she would work on Sunday, time and a half, she explained, and we don't open till half-past ten. Staff arrived at ten o'clock. Jan, who had nothing else to do on this long, idle day, readily agreed. Mrs. Allan had refrained from warning her that she would be expected to act as waitress. Irma, the regular assistant, refused Sunday work, and a "help" came on that morning. But Mrs. Banks didn't wait; she had no objection to obliging behind the scenes but equally she had no intention of any of her friends watching her demean herself by carrying cups and plates to strangers.

"It's quite simple," Mrs. Allan said. "We don't get a big clientele, but we have our regulars who come here most days, and it encourages them to know we're open on a Sunday when so many of the restaurants of our type are closed."

The Dolls' House had an enormous plate-glass window in which were exposed various comestibles for sale. All Home-made, said the hand-written cards, and since the cook was more than competent and everything was fresh, they did quite a sharp sale on Sundays in pudding, cakes and buns. At first all went well. Jan quickly got the hang of the job and the Sunday customers were in no hurry. Mostly they were elderly folk without family ties and it was pleasant to drop in, many of them after attending one of the two churches that flanked the café, and find a familiar face or two. One or two even referred to it as the Sunday Club.

At about half-past twelve Jan had such a scare she thought she would faint. Indeed, the blood receded from her face, and she almost dropped a tray she was carrying. A man had paused outside and for that anguished moment she thought it was Pat. She had no doubt at all that he was there on her account. Then he pushed open the door and she turned sharply to see Mrs. Allan watching her. Hurriedly she handed the contents of the tray to the customer who had ordered them, and when she looked up Mrs. Allan was composedly taking the newcomer's order. And it wasn't Pat. It wasn't even particularly like him, just a similar height and build. But the mischief had been done. Danger, that she had held off for the past four-and-twenty hours, came galloping up to thunder on the door, her mind was no longer on the work, she confused orders, kept stealing fearful glances at the street. Mrs. Allan made no comment until the blind was drawn down and the tables stripped ready for Monday's trade. Then she gave Jan the money due to her saying, "You've been very useful, but it was only a stopgap. I shan't be wanting you again."

Jan stared. "What did I do wrong?"

"My dear, don't be naïve. Try and see it from my point of view. This isn't the Ritz or the Savoy, we can't afford trouble even on a minor scale. You've seen the kind of clients we have, the sort who're driven away by a hint of anything out of the straight."

"I don't know what you mean," muttered Jan.

"I'm not asking any questions, I don't even want you to tell me anything. I don't know who you're running away from, a husband or the police, but any girl who looks over her shoulder as you do every time a door opens has got something to hide. In any case, you've never done this kind of work before, so why not go back to your original job?"

"I told you—I'm an actress." Jan tried to throw a note of conviction into her voice.

"Aren't we all?" Mrs. Allan sounded good-humored but quite firm. "An actress, a professional one, would know how to cover up, it would be automatic. I don't want anyone coming in here to start breaking china or making a scene. I daresay you've had bad luck and, if so, I'm sorry for you. I can't say more. I've got myself to think of. I'm a deserted wife with no alimony, this shop is my living . . ."

Jan took the money and fled. Tomorrow, she thought, she would start looking for work in another district. Pat couldn't search through every London suburb. She was perfectly convinced he was on the lookout for her.

Falcon Moor was a development site just inside the Green Belt. Here an enterprising speculator called Hart was putting up bungalows and two-storied blocks of maisonettes faster than the purchasers would be able to knock them down, and that was saying something, declared his irate competitors. Hart knew what they were saying. It made him laugh.

His men, who were paid a shade over the union rate, worked all through the week end, and he was there to make sure that if there was a bit of a drizzle they didn't settle down in the empty flats with packs of cards and tea. If his flats could stand up to a shower, so could the men who built them, who might expect a considerably longer material tenancy. He was always on hand at the week end to interview prospective buyers; he had a model flat on view, and his advertisements said mortgages arranged, which added a bit more grist to the mill.

On that particular Sunday morning a young couple called Benson—she expecting Benson Junior before Christmas—came to inspect a house and found a good deal more than they had anticipated. Madge Benson, who had lost a young brother playing on the railway lines a year earlier, wasn't sure about being so close to the track. True, there would be a garden one day, when a bulldozer had been at work on the strips of ground stretching between the houses and the line, but a lively youngster would make small work of the enclosing fence.

"Oh, there's a thundering great ditch on the further side of the fence," Mr. Hart told her in his jolly, booming voice. (Hart by name and hearty by nature was one of his standing jokes, and only someone as simple-minded as Arthur Crook would have found that amusing.) "No kid's going to be able to bridge that."

Still doubtful, the Bensons went to look for themselves. And that was how they came to be the first to find the body.

It was sprawled in the ditch among the long, coarse grass, lying on its face, a man in a dark suit, with dark hair, lying very still.

Madge said fearfully, "What on earth's he doing there?" but of course they both knew. He couldn't be hiding, because there were only two ways he could have got there; either he'd come through the estate, in which case he must have been seen, since the place was furnished with a night watchman to stop hooliganism, or he'd fallen from a train.

It was the young husband who said, "Opened the wrong door, I suppose. In the dark he mightn't see. Don't take on, Madge. He can't hurt you."

"He's dead, isn't he?" Even her voice shivered.

"Well, I don't suppose he's lying there for fun. Come on, darling, we'll leave this to Hart. It's not our job."

"It's no more his than ours. I mean, he's not on the estate, actually."

He gentled her over the lumpy ground back to where Mr. Hart was expatiating on the virtues of his dwellings to some newcomers.

"It was an accident," he soothed her.

"I suppose so. I suppose he fell last night. Only it does seem odd, Johnny. I mean, it's not very near a station. Why was he preparing to alight so early? I suppose the door could have been not properly closed. . . ."

Mr. Hart reacted badly when the Bensons burst into the little office where he was interviewing two other prospective buyers.

"Be with you in a minute," he promised cheerily, but Madge couldn't keep still.

"There's a dead man on the other side of the fence. We think he fell out of a train."

There was a sound like tearing silk as five people drew in their breath simultaneously.

"Nonsense," said Mr. Hart. "Some chap having a bit of shut-eye."

"In a ditch with the trains roaring past all day?" suggested Johnny Benson. "Be your age. The chap's dead. You'd better ring the police, hadn't you?"

Mr. Hart wriggled. He hadn't seen the corpse. . . . "I'm a doctor," said one of the prospective owners. "I'll take a look if you like."

The other husband said he'd come, too, and the wives promised to look after Madge.

"This isn't going to do me any good," grumbled Mr. Hart.

"Too bad the dead man didn't think of that," retorted Johnny. "Come to that, he doesn't seem to have done himself much good either."

"How about a cup of tea?" proposed one of the wives brightly. "There must be plenty on the site, with all these chaps at work."

It nearly broke the speculator's heart. A good half-hour wasted and lucky if it wasn't more.

It was obvious even to Johnny, who hadn't got the doctor's experience of corpses, that the chap in the ditch was as dead as the proverbial doornail.

"Seems to have fallen with an almighty whump," said the third husband. "Must have hit his head on something."

The doctor squatted companionably on his haunches. "Point is, what? The grass is as thick as the moss in a baby's coffin, and there's no convenient tree stump to account for the injury. And another thing, when a man feels he's falling his instinct is to clutch at something. This fellow's hands are folded under the body. My guess is we have to thank our old friend the blunt instrument, but that's the police's job, not ours."

The word *murder* was written as clearly in the air as if a plane had scrawled it in letters of white across the sky.

The police agreed with the doctor. Another odd circumstance was the absence of any mark of identification on the body. No wallet, no laundry marks on the clothes, no letters, not so much as a railway ticket. The clothes, that had all been bought off the hook, were creased and stained. Age thirty-two to thirty-five, decided Inspector Frost, in charge of the case; wears his own teeth, two gold fillings—that might help if we had any notion where he came from; never did manual work, look at his hands. Wonder if there's any unclaimed luggage at Paddington that might link up.

Paddington couldn't help. No unclaimed luggage, beyond a brief case which contained an identity document and had already been inquired for, had been handed in. No inquiry had come through the Missing Persons Bureau that could possibly apply to the dead man. The obvious solution was that he'd been murdered for his wallet, though why the thief hadn't helped himself to the wrist watch as well was anybody's guess.

The position of the body showed that the dead man had been traveling into London, and passengers coming back in the evening would be comparatively scanty. Landladies, during the summer season, insisted on letting rooms from Saturday to Saturday, said rooms to be vacated by midday. Most of the families, being burdened with luggage, arranged to travel back on the morning train. There was a less popular London-bound train that would pass this spot between 9:00 and 9:30 P.M., when work on the site was over and a body might be toppled into the ditch without attracting much attention. It had been fairly well concealed by grass and brambles and weeds, so it was not altogether surprising no one had noticed anything. On Saturday the advent of breakfast, morning coffee and lunch would occupy the attention of travelers on the train. The authorities knew that when people are embarking on a journey of some hours' duration they are inclined to keep their places for the first hour or so, unless, of course, food is served, and that occupies all their attention. So it didn't disconcert them to realize that Sunday's excursion train travelers hadn't spotted the body.

The news got a small paragraph in the Monday papers. MYSTERY MAN ON LINE. Jan saw the heading at the Corner Café where she was having breakfast, but her thoughts were filled with the idea of finding a job as far from Paddington as possible, and even if she had read it she would not have associated it with Pat. Like all the other *Record* readers, like the railway authorities and the police, she supposed the body must have fallen from the train on Saturday. She turned to the Appointments Vacant column and marked one or two possible advertisements.

Down at Falcon Moor the matter naturally attracted a lot more attention; during the morning a Mrs. Fletcher, living in a house close by, walked into the police station carrying a dark felt hat that, she said, her little boys had found on the line on Saturday morning. There was nothing special about it, no name, no means of identification, and she had put it to one side. They had wanted to play with it, but she thought it might do for her husband, who was a smart dresser when he could afford it. "It must be a good one," she insisted, "because look at the way it's dried. It was soaking when the boys brought it in, but I stuffed it with newspaper and then took a warm iron to it"—she had been in tailoring before she married Fletcher—"and then it seemed too good for the kids to play with.

"It did seem as if it might tie up with that body they found at Falcon Moor," she said. "If the chap was leaning out of the window and his hat blew off he might make a grab, and if the door wasn't properly shut, or somehow he dislodged the handle, well, that might explain how he came to be lying there."

The police thanked her very much; they didn't add that it wouldn't explain why he was traveling without money or papers, or how he got that bang on the back of the head. They hadn't yet released to the press their conviction that this was a case of foul play. The hat, in fact, was to provide them with a valuable clue—the first they had—for in the sweatband, tucked neatly away where Mrs. Fletcher hadn't discovered them, they found two railway tickets. These were singles from St. Benyons to Paddington and had been bought on the Friday.

"Well," said Frost, "that puts a different complexion on things. Among other things, it explains why his clothes were in such a mess. It rained like stink Friday night. Of course, the sun on Saturday and Sunday did quite a good drying job, but that couldn't restore the shape."

Now they knew that the man hadn't been traveling alone. That was one important point. And, assuming the hat was his, they also knew where he'd boarded the train. Inquiries now shifted to St. Benyons where they tracked down the booking clerk, the lady in the refreshment bar and the local porter. The last-named only remembered a crazy red-headed traveler who had jumped the train just as it was moving out, but the other two proved more coöperative. The booking clerk was pretty sure he recalled the couple, had heard the man say something about getting a cup of tea. The refreshment lady with the near-mauve hair also remembered the red-headed man —must have been asked to put out his light during the black-out, she remarked succinctly—and said he had spoken to a girl who was with a man, but she didn't remember the latter. The girl had looked dazed and the redhead, who looked like an orang-utan or something, had butted in just as if he was Khrushchev, giving orders like nobody's business. The couple had crossed the line for the London train, she never heard them speaking to each other, she couldn't be expected to remember everyone who bought a cup of tea. And so on—and so on.

"You remember the redhead all right," the police challenged her, and she said you'd have to be blind and deaf to miss him.

Then the police got a bonus they hadn't anticipated. There was any amount of talk locally, of course, and Capability Jane wasn't the kind of girl to linger timidly on the edge of any crowd. She came charging into the station with a huge half-grown dog on a chain to tell them what had happened to her on that night. Sergeant Bones, who was on duty, found it difficult to disentangle fact from fiction. For instance, she said she was certain the man was a foreigner.

"Did he speak with an accent?"

"Only a foreigner would deliberately attack a dumb beast that had done him no harm."

Then she said he was clearly intoxicated.

"Was his speech thick?"

"If he wasn't a foreigner, he must have been drunk to behave as he did."

"Could you give a description of him?"

The description tallied very well with the one they'd received of the dead man, and later she identified him—though without confirmation from Mrs. Jenkins, his landlady, that wouldn't have cut much ice. She didn't take much notice of the girl, small and dark, she thought vaguely, not quite sure, it seemed, if it was her hair or her skin that was dark. No, she wouldn't know her again.

Information now came in like an inflowing tide. London produced a record of a girl who had paid a single fare from Wakebridge, who had left the train that night; she had carried a suitcase and been unaccompanied. No one else had paid for a ticket who had come from that train. There was no proof that it was the same girl, and Wakebridge wasn't St. Benyons, but the police were at one with Arthur Crook on this point. They let it be known they were anxious to trace the girl in question. But she didn't surface.

P. C. Tedd was on a week's leave at Daisycombe when the case broke. He instantly recalled the couple in the telephone booth and went round to the local station, where he signed a statement. The description of the pair tallied with all the information in the possession of the police, the time was right, and he was the first witness to produce any sort of evidence that they were dealing with a married couple. The girl had been wearing gloves, so he could give no evidence about a wedding ring. On the face of it, it seemed probable that the wife was making a bolt for it, and been followed and overtaken by the husband. On the other hand, P. C. Tedd, a local man, didn't recall seeing the man before—though, he added, the girl's face was vaguely familiar. Why didn't he either drag her home by the hair of her head or say good riddance to bad rubbish? P. C. Tedd demanded. He had her baggage, he could just have gone home. Only she'd made it clear she wasn't going with him.

"If she had any reason to be afraid of him she had her chance to state her case," said Tedd pontifically. "If the law wasn't good enough for her . . ."

It was Miss Malpas who sewed up the job. She was an indifferent reader of newspapers, had given up the ones from London, she said, because they never gave you anything but news, and you could get that in a more succinct form on the radio. News to her only qualified for the name if it concerned the royal family or someone she had met. But she bought the local paper, because that was concerned with her small, immediate world. And so within the hour she was on the telephone to the authorities, giving them their first actual identification of the pair. Then she came plunging into the station in a black and yellow blanket coat that made her look for all the world like an outsize wasp. Crook would have taken off his brown bowler to her on sight. He knew these old girls have a habit of adding two and two and making it ninety-six, and, when you finished your sums, you found ninety-six was the right answer all along.

"And a few minutes after the girl had disappeared," she continued impressively, believing like most of her sex that the postscript's the most important part of the letter, "I heard the next-door gate slam and a man came rushing out and tore after her."

Yes, she said, of course he was following her, he turned into the alley, and the only place the alley led to was the station. And though she'd sat at her window until eleven o'clock he hadn't come back. Reluctantly, she couldn't put a name to him, but obviously he hadn't been in St. Benyons long.

Mrs. English gave the girl's name as Janice Grey; she knew nothing of her private affairs, she didn't examine her lodgers' letters or listen to their telephone calls. She had to admit Janice had disappeared very suddenly and without notice, and there hadn't been a cheep out of her since she went. She knew nothing of any man next door. After all, decent women with a living to earn, etc. etc.

Lucille also knew her as Miss Grey; she had answered an advertisement, had said she had been living in London but wanted to get away, as who wouldn't. She had been secretary-receptionist to a doctor who had emigrated. She didn't talk about herself much, never spoke of boys. Well, some girls were like that and people's private lives belonged to themselves. She was well liked and never wanted you to be sorry for her or tried to borrow money. It had been a great shock when she hadn't turned up as usual on the Monday morning, but if the police were inquiring for her, you really couldn't be surprised. They were probably wrong anyway. One of the assistants remembered her going up to London once or twice of a Saturday but who to meet couldn't tell you. No one had asked her about her business, no one really cared. When you had clients going blah blah blah under the drier all day you started to wish you lived in a world of dumb people.

The police, plodding from one address to the next, weren't making much headway until they called on Mrs. Jenkins who, for a few days, had been Pat's landlady. He'd turned up with a little case, asked for a room, paid the week in advance and made no trouble. He'd put a note in the hall before he left, explaining he'd been suddenly called away—no, she couldn't say if he'd had a phone call, she had other things to do. He'd left his luggage and said he'd be calling back. She showed it to them, one of the zip-over bags that were all the go nowadays, a suit on a hanger, more or less the twin of the one he'd been wearing, underclothes, socks, slippers, that could have belonged to anyone of a similar build. No letters, no papers of any kind. He'd signed the visitors' book P. Thompson, though, and that she did think a bit queer, because when he took his wallet out to pay the week in advance she couldn't help seeing it bore the initials P.W.W. Still, no concern of hers, the notes were O.K., and it wasn't a crime to call yourself something else, not unless it was with criminal intent. No doubt he had his reasons and it didn't pay to be nosy. The wallet had been good quality black leather—morocco, she thought. No, she couldn't be wrong about the initials; no, he hadn't had any letters so far as she could tell; no visitors; he hadn't told her what he was doing in St. Benyons, perhaps he was having a holiday.

As to the wallet, he could have bought it second-hand somewhere, couldn't he? Or he might have inherited it from an uncle.

Naturally, she couldn't help about relatives and she knew nothing about his job.

When the police left Mrs. Jenkins' house they ran against Miss Malpas coming out of the photo shop. As the witness who had supplied the name of the missing girl she thought it probable the police would want a picture of herself, and out of forty-eight poses there must be one that would reproduce satisfactorily.

They had one more visitor. This was Frank James, who came storming in to know if they'd found the girl.

"We shall," said the police.

"I'll tell you one thing, when you do you'll find she's in the clear. Why, she's not much bigger than a kitten, she couldn't kill a full-sized man."

"Wherever did you get the idea that the lady's under suspicion?" inquired the policeman blandly. "She's only got to come forward and help us. Save us a lot of trouble, too. Makes you wonder why she doesn't."

Six

The police released all this information to the press—if they hadn't, Mrs. Jenkins and Miss Malpas would have done the job for them—and that brought Edgar Barrett into the limelight. As soon as he heard about the missing wallet he realized that he could tell the police where to look for it. He had too much sense to mention the matter to his wife, who had the normal virtuous citizen's conviction that sensible people stay away from the police, so during his lunch hour he went into the nearest station and told them what he knew. He said he hadn't spoken of it to anyone, not realizing it was of any special importance. He begged them not in any circumstances to visit him at his home.

"My wife," he explained, "very sensitive."

"I understand, sir," said the station sergeant, who was on the ball-and-chain himself. They took down his office number and said they'd get a man to search the site. He could tell them roughly where he'd left the wallet, but promised to call in on his way back and, if it hadn't been found, do a personally conducted tour. Later in the day he got a message that the wallet had been found and they wanted him to call in at his local station to identify it and make a statement.

"There aren't likely to be two," he protested, but he went along just the same.

When they showed him the wallet he looked a bit taken aback.

"What is it?" said the officer sharply. "You admit yourself there aren't likely to be two."

"Oh, it's the same wallet, only it looks as if it's come in for a bit of rough handling. I remember noticing it had been given good care, except where the cat had roughed it up a bit. Now it looks—well . . ."

"It rained last night," said the policeman.

"I suppose so." Then suddenly up came his head. Slow but sure, that was Eddie Barrett. "Do you realize what you've just said?"

"I beg your pardon, sir?"

"When I found it, it hadn't been out in the rain. But it pelted on Friday night, the night this chap fell from the train or was chucked out or whatever it was, so it can't have been put on the site till Saturday."

That presented a bit of a poser, because, if you tip a chap into a ditch, having made pretty certain he won't be able to get up again, you want to rid yourself of the incriminating evidence as soon as possible. There's always the one-in-a-thousand chance that the body will be found quite soon, and then the heat will be on. There must have been opportunities to get rid of the wallet that same night, either out of the window a bit nearer London or on some building site near the station. But X seemed to have hung onto the wallet till the next day. Yet it had been discarded before the body was found, so it wasn't a case of chucking it away when it became obvious it might be dangerous to keep it. And whoever had got rid of it either lived in the neighborhood of the car cemetery or had to pass it on the way home.

The obvious answer was that the wallet hadn't been found till the Saturday, in which case the finder was most probably one of the railway cleaners. The train had not gone out again until eight o'clock on Saturday morning; the police patiently interviewed all the available cleaners, none of whom admitted any knowledge of the wallet and several of whom were mightily indignant at this slur on their integrity. The only one they couldn't trace was Raikes, who had gone on leave. He had not been employed on this job for very long and no one seemed to know much about him. They had his home address, of course, but when they beetled around there his landlady told them he'd gone and wouldn't be coming back.

"Fed up with the job," she said, "and not liking London anyway."

They asked how much notice he'd given and she put her hands on her hips and laughed.

"They don't know what the word means. That's why I always ask for a week in advance. Not that there's any trouble letting rooms these days. I had a girl in the same afternoon. Over from Ireland. Come without any idea where they're going to sleep, like cuckoos."

"Did you notice whether he seemed particularly flush of cash?"

She gave them a pitying glance. "He was going on his holiday, wasn't he? No, I didn't ask him where he was going. It doesn't pay to be nosy. What you don't know isn't any concern of yours."

All this good breeding, snorted Crook, when he heard. "Oh no, Constable, I never look over the fence into my neighbor's garden. How was I to know he was being strangled by a great big python? I didn't put it there." And being British, they'd probably argue that the python had a point of view, too—it's a free country, isn't it, and who were they to interfere?

In crime, it often turns out that the most obvious solution is the true one, and when a chap's found heaved out of a train with a nasty smash on the back of his head and his wallet gone, nine times out of ten it's a case of robbery with more violence than was originally intended, but somehow that didn't seem the answer here. Because if Raikes had found an empty wallet he'd have handed it in with the brief case and mackintosh; and in any case, even an amateur thief wouldn't have left the wallet in the carriage. Then they got what seemed the prize tie-up; inquiries at Somerset House produced the record of a girl called

Janice Grey marrying a man named Patrick William Wylie rather more than two years before. So all that remained now was to find Mrs. Wylie and ask her for her explanation.

The police were not the only people anxious to trace her. In a flat in Pimlico three men were on the same lay. The one who seemed to be the chief was a big fellow, as ugly as an ape and as dangerous as a rattler. One of the others was a tall, rather thin man who'd look like a thousand others if you saw him in uniform. The third was small and dark and had trouble written all over him.

"This is a hell of a situation," stormed the big man. "I told you the thing was to look like an accident. Everything was laid on, darkness, an empty train, more or less, and the girl out of the way. And you had to muff it with both of them."

"You make it sound as easy as kiss your hand," the tall man grumbled. "How was I to guess the fool had left his wallet in the carriage?"

"If you'd frisked the carriage you'd have found it," his boss insisted.

"I hadn't got all the time in the world, the girl could have come back at any minute. And we were getting close to the Junction. I chucked out his hat, he hadn't a bag, only the case the girl brought with her."

"It would have shown more sense to wait for her to come back," the other man grumbled. "But no, you had to play it smart, go stalking along the corridor, and be caught."

"He didn't see me, I can swear to that. And time was running out."

"It should have looked like an accident, any chap can fall leaning out of the window too far, but now the cops know there's something fishy afoot. You can't imagine the girl will keep her lip buttoned about all this."

"She hasn't surfaced, that might mean something."

"Well, she's got to be found before the police get onto her. You'd better get cracking right away. Odds are she'll lie low in London. Paddington's honeycombed with lodging houses. You'll have to organize a house-to-house enquiry."

The third man, the shortish dark one, said, "You'd wonder she hasn't gone to the police herself, asked for protection."

"And have them ask her how it was that, when she was traveling alone with her husband, he managed to fall out of a train, minus his wallet, and she didn't report him as missing? Everyone knows that when there's a sudden death in the family it's the next of kin who're the first to be put on the spot. Not that Pat's any loss," he added viciously. "Once he left his job and couldn't get us the inside story any more, he was no more use to us than a sick headache. Couldn't even take orders, knew it all first. I told him—put this chap out for a few hours, that's all, but no, he has to use his discretion, whatever that may be, and put him down for the count."

"Pat wasn't to know he had an abnormally thin skull," said the small dark man. "Knowles 'ud swing manslaughter on the evidence."

"Forgetting the cops have got a watch out on account of that other idiot who croaked? No, they'd like to see us all swing and the fact that it was Pat did the job won't help us much."

"There's something else," the dark man said. "The girl knew more than was healthy about those other cases; that makes her accessory after the fact. Why should anyone believe her story about being attacked on the train? No, she'll go underground and stay there till she has to come up for breath. Our one hope is to be on the spot when she does surface. It's all a question of which of us gets there first."

It was that pair of ancient harpies, Arsenic and Old Lace, who most improbably set the police on the new track. It was the most profitable conversation they'd had with anyone for years. Not only did they help to shift the burden of suspicion from Jan's shoulders, they actually indicated the neck round which it should be slung. Not, of course, that they had the remotest idea they were doing anything of the kind.

When he first saw them, fearfully and wonderfully arrayed in their Sunday-go-to-meeting bibs and tuckers, the station sergeant, who had a literary bent, thought, Two of the witches from the blasted heath. Wonder what's happened to the third.

With one voice they demanded an audience with the Chief Inspector, claiming exclusive information in "the train outrage." The police, who were being inundated with letters, telephone calls and even visits from every sort of lunatic, some of whom hadn't been within a hundred miles on the night in question, stalled them till it became obvious that this couple had actually been on the murder train, and could give information—eye-witness information, insisted Arsenic severely—that so far hadn't been made public. So eventually they were taken along to see Inspector Frost. And for the first time the police learned of a remarkable encounter between the missing girl—or someone who tallied with their description of Janice Grey—and an unknown man who resembled nothing so much as an orang-utan.

"My friend even thought of ringing up the zoo to enquire if one had escaped," contributed Old Lace humorously. But the joke fell a bit flat. Even Arsenic would have known better than that; she gave her companion a quelling glance that made the inspector think of his mother-in-law.

"It's perfectly obvious what happened," she announced. "This man was responsible for Patrick Wylie's death, and the girl was an unexpected witness of the attack. So, naturally, she had to be silenced, and if I hadn't had to come through from my carriage to the one in which the Wylies were traveling, I daresay he'd have succeeded."

Old Lace chipped in with something about the failure of British Railways to recognize their obligations to first-class passengers, but once again Arsenic sent her an annihilating glance.

No, she agreed in reply to the inspector, she'd no more absolute proof than what she had already provided, "but, goodness me," she protested, "isn't that enough? The facts speak for themselves."

"Whereabouts did this attack take place?" Frost wanted to know.

"I told you, in the corridor."

"I mean, at what stage of the journey?"

"The train had just emerged from the tunnel before reaching Cranley Junction."

That meant, of course, that the attack on Pat had already

been made and he was either dead or lying unconscious by the side of the track. What bothered them was that the red-headed man hadn't come forward with his story, but the answer to that could well be that Arsenic's theory was the correct one. It was always possible, of course, that her yarn was a complete invention, but Frost didn't think so. There was the disquieting confirmation by the lady in the St. Benyons refreshment room, who had noticed a red-headed man speaking to the girl, and the porter who remembered him leaping on board the train just as it was drawing out.

Still, there was no harm asking a few more questions.

"If Miss Grey saw her husband being attacked, isn't it strange she didn't shout for help or pull the communication cord?" he suggested.

"It's news to me that there are communication cords in the corridor," replied Arsenic, at her iciest. "As for shouting, there were very few people on board the train and the noise it was making would probably have drowned her voice in any case."

"Is there any proof that she was, in fact, in the corridor when the attack took place?—the attack on her husband, I mean," seeing Arsenic preparing to launch another poisoned dart.

"I had to wait several minutes in the corridor while this girl made up her face, if that's the right expression, in the toilet compartment."

"And you think that while she was there Patrick Wylie was murdered? In that case, why should this strange man have attacked her, since she couldn't conceivably have been an eyewitness?"

Arsenic was floored, but only for a moment. "Then presumably she saw him leave her husband's carriage, and would later be able to identify him."

"It certainly clears her," the inspector acknowledged. "She can't have been making up her face and attacking her husband at one and the same time."

The Falcon Moor Estate was not more than three minutes distance from the near end of the tunnel, so the time factor alone seemed to save Jan. Only, of course, these old dears have pretty elastic notions about time; several minutes might mean no more than ninety seconds. Still, the red-headed chap had to come from somewhere.

"As for your second question," Arsenic continued, looking like Queen Victoria's youngest cousin, "the poor creature was paralyzed by fright. Half-suffocated, too. That's why I didn't see her face more clearly. This man had his immense hand over it." She shuddered, remembering there had been hairs—so revoltingly masculine. "Of course, he pretended to be succoring her, actually tried to snatch my bag, Inspector."

"Oh no," groaned the inspector. He had enough on his plate without this type of side issue. All these old girls were the same, had minds like Clapham Junction, that go all ways at once.

"It seems a particularly unwise place to choose," he commented. "There are usually people going in and out of the toilet compartment most of the journey."

"We were nearing a station," pointed out Arsenic delicately. "That would be the one time when most people would be in their carriages collecting their luggage."

"Only if they were going to alight at the next station."

"In any case, there is a notice asking that the toilet compartment should be unoccupied when the train is not in motion. Besides, I expect he didn't anticipate meeting the girl, or else she put up more of a fight than he expected. I can tell you what she looked like, small and dark, her hair done in that kind of beehive that's so fashionable—"

Old Lace giggled. "I always say if those girls ever lost anything they'd only have to take their hair down to find it."

"Really, Alice," exclaimed Arsenic. "This is a police station. About twenty-two, I'd say," she added, turning back to Frost. "Wore a dark coat and these silly high-heeled shoes, but I couldn't give you any very definite details."

"I see. Thank you, madam. Anything else you remember about the man?"

"Middle-aged, heavily built, a very common-looking person, wearing quite dreadful clothes. And his voice." She shuddered again.

"You hadn't seen him before—on the train, I mean?"

"Clearly he had been traveling at the rear end. We were in the middle, that's where the first-class coach was. But after I had got back and was telling my friend what had happened—after we had stopped at Cranley Junction, that is—I saw him go by the window, obviously making for his own carriage."

"So he came on to London. It seems odd the young lady didn't make a charge." He frowned.

"Perhaps she was in a state of shock. She doesn't even appear to have noticed her husband had disappeared."

"Perhaps," suggested Old Lace brilliantly, "she also had something to hide."

"Or perhaps he got her at Paddington Station," contributed Arsenic, not to be outdone.

The police had been hard at work tracking down Pat's past, and they had little doubt that he had been associated with a gang of jewel thieves who had brought off some remarkable coups during the past three or four years, and were in all probability responsible for the latest burglary in which a man called Routh had been so badly injured that he had died. They noted that it was only after this that Wylie had contacted his wife, and doubtless she would be a danger to the other members of the gang, assuming she'd ever met any of them. They wished for more information about the mysterious redhead, not guessing, of course, how soon he was going to surface.

Frost stood up and politely thanked the ladies for their trouble and very valuable information; and he hadn't got his tongue in his cheek when he said that. It was about the first useful news that had come their way.

And then, just as she turned to go, Arsenic dropped her bombshell.

"You know what they say—when you need a policeman he's never there. There was no sign of the guard on the train, I suppose he was engaged in some other part of it. We saw no one except the ticket collector, and even he didn't bother us."

Old Lace smirked. "They can always tell, can't they?"

"Tell what?" asked Frost.

"The kind who travel first-class on second-class tickets."

"You mean, he just walked past the window?"

"Yes."

"Did you hear him go into any of the other compartments?"

"Well, really, Inspector, there was practically no one else in our part of the train."

"Do you remember when it was that he went by?"

"Yes," said Old Lace. "We were wondering if he might be coming, and then he went past and my friend said she thought she'd run along and freshen up. Since he clearly wasn't going to bother about clipping our tickets."

"Perhaps he'd been along earlier," Frost suggested.

But both ladies vetoed that at once.

"Oh no. We got on at the terminus."

"It didn't strike you as odd that he didn't ask to see your tickets."

Arsenic threw her head so high it looked as though she'd never catch it when it came down.

"We didn't think about it."

"And I don't suppose you happened to notice his appearance?"

They both looked rather huffed. "Naturally not. He was a ticket collector."

"Well," said Frost, "you've been the greatest possible help. You won't mind if we get in touch with you again later?"

And receiving their gracious assurances that they wouldn't mind at all, he watched them sail out.

"So it was as simple as that," mused Frost to his sergeant when they had departed. "Fancy that pair putting us on the rails. You see, according to official records, there was no ticket collector on that train."

It wouldn't, they decided, have been difficult to work. X would board the train wearing usual mufti duds and carrying a suitcase. Inside the suitcase would be the usual ticket taker's blue overcoat and peaked cap. A gang would have no difficulty in obtaining them. Chaps who can make a getaway with several thousand pounds' worth of jewels aren't going to be stymied when it comes to a simple bit of foxing of that description. He'd await his opportunity and when the girl left Wylie alone that would be his chance. The front part of the train, in which the couple had traveled, had been very sparsely filled, the train was approaching a tunnel—it was a risk, of course, but one the gang presumably considered worth-while. It looked as though Pat was the weak link in their chain, the man responsible for Routh's death, or else considered most likely to break down if it came to police interrogation. Might even have turned Queen's Evidence. They had learned that Jan left her husband just after the Cadogan Terrace affair, in which a man also had died.

"It could be they were afraid of her going to the police," said Frost. "The news of Routh's death was only in the papers that night, but presumably the gang would be keeping in touch. One wonders what their plan for her was. They could hardly hope to put two corpses on the railway track, and I daresay they hoped Wylie's death would be attributed to accident."

"It was a bit of luck about the wallet . . ."

"And the hat. You know what they say about the wicked man flourishing like a green bay tree, Somers? Ah, but the bay tree can never be certain when some fellow won't come along with an axe and chop, chop, chop it down."

It hadn't escaped their attention that no inquiries had been made about Pat, no relatives had called at the mortuary, the only visitors had been the occasional distracted man or woman coming to see if he or she could identify the body, and of course never able to do so. The girl might be lying low through sheer terror, or she might hope that no one would associate her with Pat's wife, now Pat's widow. There's no limit to the hoperation women allow themselves, as both Crook and the inspector could testify.

They circulated a description of the red-headed man, but Arsenic hadn't been able to tell them much. Still, someone else might have remembered noticing him, though the average British traveler could sit next to a chimpanzee and notice nothing until the brute started clawing his hair. And when the train was so empty, the odds were the chap could get a carriage to himself. It was even possible that the spurious ticket collector and the red-headed man were one and the same person.

Jan realized it was going to be a neck-and-neck race between her and the two separate packs who were on her trail—thugs and police. The obvious thing was to move again as quickly as possible. They would both know she had alighted at Paddington fairly late in the evening and would presumably look for a room in that neighborhood. At the Corner Café she scanned the small ads in the *Record,* looking for some job where she might be acceptable without references. There only appeared to be two possibilities. She could return to dish-washing or become an usherette at a suburban cinema. One company was asking for usherettes at three of their houses. Good wages. Experience not necessary. The advantage of working in a cinema was that, though you mixed with the public, you were in the dark most of the time; and if she took a job in one of the remoter districts it was long odds against Harris or even the police smoking her out there.

One of the districts listed in the ads was Neston Way and, emerging from the café, she saw a bus with this direction on the front, so she climbed on board, the newspaper folded under her arm.

Seven

The bus journey, scheduled for forty minutes, took fifty, thanks to the traffic. The road ran through every kind of neighborhood, handsome modern blocks of flats and stores giving way, as the vehicle turned a corner, to grim narrow brick Victorian houses, where the prams stood wheel-deep in weeds in the small, untended gardens, and cats crouched and pounced like their bigger brethren in the jungle. Surely in this wilderness, she reflected, hope rising in her heart again, there must be some obscure hole where one small girl could lie hidden.

Neston Way bristled with television masts so that it would not have been surprising to see a harbor beyond the houses. The cinema was tall, shabby and clearly would shortly give way to a hall for bingo, billiards or rock-and-roll. The manager was a tired-looking man counting the years to his pension; he didn't query her story, which didn't mean that he believed it. Girls without references told him every sort of yarn. But it didn't matter to him. It was a dead-end job in any case, and few of the usherettes lasted long. They had nothing to do with the takings and it was improbable that a skilled pickpocket would waste time in Neston Way. The girl looked clean and intelligent and had pleasant manners. He gave her about a month before something better turned up. It was even possible that she was on the stage, though only just on it, the smallest push would send her back into the wings; he engaged her at once, and while she was on the spot she thought she better look for a room. It was much harder getting somewhere to live than somewhere to work; she walked up and down steps, opened and closed gates, till she felt her knees would give under her, but by four o'clock she was accepted as the tenant of an indifferent-looking room in a house in a side street. She agreed to come in the following day. When she got back to Paddington she saw the flaring headlines in the afternoon editions—Late Night Final they were called. WHERE IS JANICE GREY? they demanded. Her heart gave a sickening jolt. Now danger yapped like a cur at her heels but even at this juncture she wasn't tempted to go to the police. Women are like that, Crook would have said. They have the idea they can outsmart Machiavelli—and sometimes, he would add with a grin, it turns out that they can.

Miss Hiscock was waiting in the hall as she let herself in.

"I wanted a word with you, Miss Graham," she said, and her bearing was as grim as her voice.

"Oh, Miss Hiscock, I've got myself a job. I have to move out tomorrow."

She followed the landlady into her own quarters at the end of a long passage. No comfort here, nothing cozy, not a bit like Mrs. English's pleasant bed-sitter with its television set and modern draperies.

"It's not actually the stage, it's a film company, and I have to start immediately," Janice ran on. "It was in the paper. I answered the advertisement, and I got the job. It's nothing very spectacular, but it's a beginning, isn't it? Well, isn't it?" she repeated, in a coaxing voice.

"The police have been here," said Miss Hiscock abruptly, and again she knew that sickening jolt at the heart.

"Not looking for me, I suppose." She must be a bit of an actress really, she thought, hearing her own voice.

"I don't know. They're looking for a girl called Janice Grey."

"Oh yes, I saw that name on the placards. I haven't had time to read the paper yet."

"You signed the visitors' book as Jane Graham."

"Why not?"

"Is that your real name?"

The girl's hand curled fiercely around the back of a chair, cold hand against cold wood.

"What an extraordinary question!"

"This Janice Grey was on your train."

"There were quite a lot of people on my train."

"They think she probably found a room in Paddington that night."

"Well, I hope she did. Why on earth are you asking me? Oh, I see. The initials. But there must be heaps of girls called—oh, Judith Green or Jessica Gardiner or—let's see—Julia Golightly . . ."

"I daresay." Miss Hiscock's expression didn't change. "They didn't all travel on that train or come looking for rooms that night. And they wouldn't all be about twenty-two and have dark hair and carry a blue suitcase."

"I can see the police have put the wind up you," Janice agreed. "Well, what would you like me to do about it?"

"I suppose you can prove your name's Jane Graham?"

Like hell she could.

"It ought to be simple enough, to prove who you really are," she conceded. "It's too bad I don't have a driving license or even a passport."

"Someone must be able to identify you. These people you were working with."

"They're scattered to the four winds, you know what a rep company is."

"I don't hold with the theater. Still, your landlady . . ."

"Yes, of course. The trouble is people on the stage so often don't use their own names." She leaned against the wall, thinking furiously. Someone had a radio playing, someone was practicing the flute.

"He's coming back in the morning. I said you'd be here."

"Did he say what time? I've got to be on this job. Do you ever go to the films?" she added frantically.

"Pack of nonsense," retorted Miss Hiscock. "Giving young people the idea that life's what they call a piece of cake. Let me tell you that there's much more dry bread than cake, and some of that's pretty stale."

"I'll tell you what," cried Janice. "Suppose I were to go down to the station after dinner?" (Supposing she did!) "I expect it's like that theater that advertises it never closes. Then they wouldn't have to come pestering you in the morning."

Miss Hiscock—she had the face of a worried Pekingese—looked startled, possibly at the notion of anyone being coöperative.

"Well, now that's an idea. You must know, Miss Graham, it doesn't do a landlady any good to have the police calling. People's consciences may be as clear as driven snow, whatever that may be, but all the same the sight of a uniform does give you a jolt. Well, dinner'll be on the stroke, and then if you were to go down . . ."

Janice smiled, a charming, conspiratorial, deceitful smile, and ran upstairs.

"I'm deliberately cheating her," she told herself, beginning to fling her possessions into the blue suitcase. "And I don't feel in the least guilty. I suppose I'm becoming a hardened criminal, but then I've been agin the law ever since I knew about Pat being mixed up with a gang and not going to the police. I don't even feel sorry for her when the police come round tomorrow. I suppose the truth is I need all the compassion I've got for myself."

She continued folding, packing, rolling stockings, stuffing shoes with newspaper. By the time she was ready to go down to dinner there was nothing left to add but what she would actually use tonight and in the morning. After dinner, her handbag swinging from her wrist, she went out.

"Little Miss Head-in-Air," muttered one of the other boarders, who had intended to make a pass at her to enliven a dull evening.

"Oh, she has what you young people call a date," Miss Hiscock assured him jauntily.

During the next forty minutes Jan sat in the little Comedy Picture House watching Mr. Magoo and Tom and Jerry and Popeye the Sailor Man. When the program started to come round again she decided she had been away long enough. Miss Hiscock was in the hall, talking to a prospective boarder, a long pale girl in a drab raincoat.

"I'll have a room free tomorrow," she was saying. Jan caught her eye and nodded.

"It's all right," she said, "everything's fixed."

Next morning she put her remaining belongings in the suitcase, counted her very small capital, wondered what she could raise on her little pearl necklace in an emergency, stripped the bed and opened the window. Then cautiously she opened the door and looked out. It occurred to her that this was the second time in a week that she had made a stealthy getaway. Thank goodness, there was no Miss Malpas here. All the doors of the house seemed closed as she came tremulously from stair to stair. She slipped through the hall like a ghost and opened the main door. An instant later she was scooting down the steps and along the sidewalk. So far as she could tell, she had left no traces, had given no hint of the district in which her new work lay, hadn't even left behind a line of apology or explanation. The Corner Café had been open for more than an hour when she went in, setting the case down by the counter.

"Usual?" asked Sally. "You getting out?"

"I've got this film job. I'll have to live more or less on the site."

"What company?"

"It's a new one, just opening, out Hendon way," she murmured vaguely, taking the cup and plate. The morning paper was featuring Pat again. The police, it seemed, were on a new trail and an early arrest, etc., etc. Jan let the paper fall. A new trail—that led straight to Miss Hiscock's door? She wondered at what time the police officer would call again and reveal the fact that no Miss Graham or Miss Anyone Else had called in at the station last night. A truck driver, coming in for a rapid cup, saw her sitting there, staring, like someone in a trance, and asked, jerking his head in her direction, "What's wrong with the young lady? Looks as if she's seen a ghost."

"Don't worry," said Sally. "She's got herself a job in the films and can't start rehearsing soon enough."

He drank the tea, standing at the counter, wiped his mouth on his hand, and went out. The door plunged open again and a party of six office cleaners surged in. They were in high spirits, chaffing and chuckling and ordering cups of tea. It was clear that they were regular customers; Jan hadn't seen them before because usually she didn't come in till later. They woke her from her trance, they were so lively and noisy and apparently free from care. They took the table behind her, squeezing in, all six of them, in a space intended for four, pushing back their chairs so that she was fenced between them and the wall. Two or three of them had newspapers and almost immediately they began to talk about Pat.

"You mark my words, that girl was in it," said one. "I mean, very convenient the way she wasn't there when he fell."

"Can't blame her really," offered the second. "Many's the time I could have pushed my old man through the window."

"You should tell him one of these days," said the third.

"Oh, he knows. That's why he'll never have a window open when he's at home."

"Men!" ejaculated the fourth.

"What's wrong with them?" a new voice demanded, a little black-haired sparrow of a woman with a light in her eye that would defy the blackout regulations.

"Oh, I don't say they're all rotten," agreed No. 1 generously. "Up to six months I've nothing against them, but after that they seem to go off."

They lighted cigarettes, they aired their views so vociferously that one of the despised men sitting nearby looked up to say, "Chuck it, girls. We can listen to all that when we're at home. We want a bit of peace here."

Jan felt like Sterne's starling. I must get out, she thought. But she was jammed against the wall. And anyway no one associated her with the missing girl. Play it down, remember what Pat said about the partridge. Half-heartedly she cut a bit off her roll.

The door opened again and a man came in. He asked for

a cup of coffee and stood looking around for a moment for an empty place. Quite a number of workmen had dropped in, the place was fuller than Jan had ever seen it. After an instant's hesitation the newcomer crossed to her table and set down his cup. It was like hearing a key turn in a lock, now you couldn't get out. She bit the roll but it was like cardboard, tasteless, sickening. She picked up the coffee cup. The man produced a cigarette case, opened it, hesitated again, and then passed it across the table.

"No, thank you," she said quickly, "but you smoke if you want to. I'm just going in any case."

"But you haven't finished your coffee, you've hardly begun it."

"I don't want any more."

"What's the hurry, Mrs. Wylie?"

She had put out her hand to pick up her bag, now she stopped, the arm in mid-air, like some freak exhibit from Madame Tussaud. She felt like a stone image, only her heart lived, and that banged and thumped until that rigid form began to shake. Slowly she drew back her hand.

"You're making a mistake," she whispered. "I don't know . . ."

"I know. You're Jane Graham and you're up from Devonshire where you've been playing in rep. What made you break your journey at St. Benyons, Miss Graham?"

"St. Benyons?"

"In a minute you're going to tell me you've never heard of Pat Wylie."

"He's the man who fell out of a train. I read about him."

"You'd better tell the sergeant about it," her companion suggested. "I mean, if you really are Jane Graham, you'll be able to prove it, won't you? But—I think you've got it wrong. I think you're Janice Grey who married Pat Wylie and I think you were with him on the train on Friday night and since then . . ."

She put her hands over her ears.

"Who are you, anyway?"

He put his hand in his pocket. "I'm a police officer," he told her, in the same unhurried voice. "You can see my warrant."

"No, no." For the first time she was grateful to the band of cleaners for making so much noise; it drowned any quieter conversation. "There's no need to let everyone see you're arresting me."

"But I'm not arresting you." He sounded surprised; he locked his hands together and let them lie idly on the surface of the table. "There's no charge. It's simply that we want your help. Well, you're not denying that the dead man is—was—your husband?"

"I didn't know," she said in the same hurried, whispering voice. "That it was Pat, I mean. I didn't know he was dead. I thought he'd just taken the money and disappeared."

"The money?"

"Yes." She told him about the sixty pounds. "We were just coming into Cranley Junction, and I thought he must have got off there. I'd gone to wash, you see, and when I came back he'd disappeared. I couldn't think why, till I opened the case and found the money had gone. I only had what was in my purse, but the relief—I'd been cudgeling my wits how to escape him, you see. I'd even had some brilliant idea about jumping off the train as it slowed up at one of the stations. But I needn't have worried." She laughed, low and jerky. "Someone tried to do that job for me."

"You must tell us all about it at the station," he said soothingly. "By the way, why didn't you report the loss when you reached Paddington?"

"Because I thought it was Pat, of course. I was so confused."

"When did you realize it couldn't have been?"

"When I heard they'd found his body. And then I thought of something else. I thought whoever had killed him was after me, too. That's why I daren't go to the police."

The man shook his head. "That doesn't make sense. The police were your natural protectors."

"You don't suppose I'd ever have been allowed to get as far as the station, do you?"

"Oh come, Mrs. Wylie, you can't seriously think this man, whoever he was, would be watching every station in London. There was the telephone, you could have rung up . . ."

"I'd no proof," she muttered. "They might have thought I was inventing it all. I wanted to stay out of the limelight. This was a desperate gang, remember."

"Oh? You knew your husband was associated with a gang?"

"That's why I left him in the first place. After the Cadogan Terrace affair a year ago . . ."

He said slowly, "A man died in that connection. It was your duty . . ."

"I'd no actual proof. I thought—yes, of course I should have come to you, but it was my husband. And now this second armed robbery . . ."

"You associate your husband and his—friends—with that, too?" He seemed startled.

"Again, I have no proof. Only—leopards don't change their spots."

"What did your husband tell you about that last affair?"

"Only that the man asked for it. He said it was just one of those things. At least, I think he meant that one. I do feel confused." Her heart was racing again. Could she be arrested and placed in the dock with the other members of the gang simply because she hadn't informed on her husband? Terrible to be twenty-two and so ignorant of common law.

"Do you know the names of any of the gang?"

"There was a heavily scarred man I saw him talking to—Pat, I mean—at Victoria Station. I think he's called Harris. I never met him. I never met any of them."

"All the same, I believe you may be able to help us, Mrs. Wylie. Now, don't be too nervous, we're not inhuman, and we can see the tangle you were in. But I'm afraid you'll have to come down to the station, the sergeant may want to ask you a few more questions. Drink your coffee. No, I'll get you another cup. That's undrinkable."

She tried to say she didn't want it, but she was shivering so much she couldn't shape the words. She even thought of trying to make a bolt for it while he stood at the counter, but that was ridiculous. He was between her and the door, and before she could grab the suitcase he'd be on her. Anyway, the cleaners, who were still whooping it up at the next table, would be the most effective barrier conceivable. She sank back in her chair. The man returned with the coffee and she put her hands gratefully around the china cup to get the warmth.

"Have you any relatives or friends, anyone you'd like to get in touch with?" he inquired. "You can ring from the station, you know."

"No," she said quickly. "No, there's no one. Anyway, I shan't need anyone. I've only got to answer a few questions, haven't I?"

"That's all. Ready? I'll take the case."

They went out and the cleaners looked at each other and grinned.

"Well, she starts pretty early in the day," said one. They tried to catch Sally's eye, pantomimed their amusement, but Sally looked glum. No sense of humor, some people, they agreed.

Around the corner from the café was a narrow street with a pub on one corner and a church on the other. Here a car was parked, a white car with a man at the wheel reading the morning paper, reading about Janice Grey, no doubt. At least, she thought, they hadn't sent a police car. She got into the back seat; she found her small handkerchief was clenched in her hand. The driver backed the car and soon they were bowling away in the direction in which she'd come. It was hard to believe that not half an hour ago she had been free to walk down this road, stop and buy her paper from the old man by the church, buy coffee, get on a bus to go on to the next chapter, and now she was on her way to be grilled by the police.

They passed a cinema, it was showing a thriller—*By Hook or Crook*—and at the sight of it, well, it was like throwing up a black window and finding the sun's shining outside after all.

"I've just remembered something," she cried. "You said I could ring up anyone I liked from the station."

"That's so."

"And isn't it the law that I can't be made to answer any questions until my lawyer's present?"

"We're not the Gestapo," the man pointed out mildly. "No one's going to hold lighted matches to the back of your neck. Have you got a lawyer then?"

"Yes. His name's Crook, Arthur Crook. Have you ever heard of him?"

"Have we ever heard of the Nelson Column? How on earth did you run against him? Or did your husband . . . ?"

"It's a funny thing, that last day in the train Pat actually mentioned him. I'd never heard of him before. And to think he was on the train—and had spoken to me at the station! Oh, only to say hadn't I better have a brandy-and-soda, but he was the one who saved my life. Fancy my forgetting him."

"You'll have to tell the sergeant about him saving your life, won't you?"

She felt a new buoyancy. "Pat says he—I mean, Pat said he never loses a client."

"You haven't been accused of anything yet," her companion reminded her dryly.

"I think I'll get him just the same. He gives you confidence just to feel he's there." She looked about her. "Aren't we taking a long time to get to the station?"

"Detour," said the man briefly.

A new fear rose in her. "You are taking me to the station? I mean, you can't take me straight to a court or—or a prison."

"The ideas you get!"

A minicar, sweeping round the corner, nearly caught them amidships; the blue case that had been placed on the front seat rocked dangerously, and instinctively she leaned forward to steady it. At the same moment the driver put out his left hand for the same purpose. It was a big hand and powerful, and there was a signet ring on one finger.

The man next to her was saying something about irresponsible drivers. Janice didn't hear him; she was doing careful mental arithmetic.

"Feeling sleepy?" he asked.

"Should I? Yes, of course. That's why you fetched the coffee."

"What do you think you're talking about?"

"Great oaks from little acorns grow." She was beginning to feel light-headed. "I mean, you can't afford to disregard even small details, can you? Someone should have reminded your driver that even off duty police don't wear rings."

"Who says they don't?"

"But the man who tried to choke me on the train wore a ring, he cut my lip. That's how I knew it wasn't Pat, he didn't wear a ring, he thought they were sissy. And, of course, that's why it isn't a police car. And I thought you were just being considerate."

Everything fell into place at once; she felt like someone being swept momentarily closer and closer to the weir.

She began to laugh; the laughter came from a long way off, as if she were listening in the next room. Clouds seemed to be swirling around in her brain, every word was another step taken in a mudbank, energy simply drained away.

"Mr. Crook," she whispered.

"Oh yes, you were going to ring him from the station."

"But we aren't going to any station." She made a feeble kind of gesture, striking out at her companion, clutching at the man in the driver's seat.

"For Pete's sake, shut that dame's mouth," he exclaimed. "It was bad enough having a mucker like Pat on the books, without having to cope with his woman as well."

"I was legally married," Janice muttered hazily. "It was all very, very legal. Somerset House—marriage lines . . ."

It was funny how the bright morning had darkened over. She'd been going to keep an appointment somewhere, she'd started early on purpose. But whoever it was would have to wait because she must—she simply must—sleep.

"Have to wait," she said, and giggled. "Going to sleep." Her head drooped.

"That's right," said the man at her side. "You say your prayers and go to sleep. Say them to Mr. Crook," he added viciously, "and you better make them good, because you're going to want all the help he can give you."

"I don't like it," said the driver a few minutes later. "Why does Harris always have to do things the hard way? What was wrong with a simple hit-and-run?"

"There's no such thing as a simple hit-and-run in London. Too many Paul Prys. Besides, we had to know what questions were likely to be asked when she didn't surface. Now we know she hasn't any family or friends, that landlady only knows her as Jane Graham, and if she does suspect her real identity she'll only think the girl's gone to ground to escape the police. And she doesn't know who attacked her in the train."

"I still don't like it," the driver insisted. "Why the hell does Crook have to be involved?"

"He's not involved. She didn't get onto him, and, take my word for it, she won't."

"You're forgetting, aren't you? Crook's no gentleman, he doesn't wait to be invited, he just comes barging in. Stand back, you blazing fool," he added, in a loud furious voice.

The elderly man, walking on a stick, who had begun laboriously to cross the street on a pedestrian crossing, stopped dead and stared, then he moved on. The driver yelled something uncomplimentary about his pedigree, swerved sharply, striking an island in the middle of the road and just got by.

"You blasted murderer!" yelled the old man, who seemed riven to the spot. His hat fell off, and someone came forward to rescue it. Two cars hooted, but the inevitable pedestrians, all hating motorists as the driver of the car hated Crook, sprang up and came to his aid.

"You should report him," said one sturdy voice.

He turned his angular yellow head. "Did you get the number? Because I didn't."

"I got it, mister." A boy of about ten hurried forward. "ARP 1951. Year I was born, see. That made me notice it. Car was a Clumber—coo, they're smashing."

"Clumber," repeated the old man, disregarding the hooting that was now taken up by several other waiting vehicles. "Don't be a fool, boy. Clumber's a dog. Bred them myself when I was a young man."

He seemed perfectly prepared to stand on the crossing for the rest of the day, recalling the golden past, when the sun had always shone and the girls had been golden, too.

A young policeman pushed his way through the crowd that had begun to assemble on the sidewalk.

"What's all this? You can't hold up the traffic, sir, even if it is a pedestrian crossing."

"Held it up a damned sight longer if that chap had knocked me down the way he meant to," said the old gentleman stoutly. "Came careering up like the charge of the Light Brigade. Ask these chaps, they saw him."

"That's right," said the boy. "I got his number—look." He had scribbled it down in a small notebook that he now offered to the law. The policeman took the old chap's arm and cleared the road, then he waved the traffic on. These crossings, he reflected, more trouble than they're worth. Pedestrians think they can saunter across as if they were at a garden party, while half the motorists don't see why they should stop for one old boy who probably isn't hurrying anywhere except the cemetery.

"How are you, sir?" he asked, depositing the old man on the opposite sidewalk. "Hurt?"

The old man fired up like a Chinese cracker. "Let me tell you, sir, I've borne arms in three wars, it takes more than a drunken driver to dispose of me. All the same, the fellow's a danger to the public. Wouldn't surprise me if that was a stolen car, what's more."

When he read the papers later in his club he said triumphantly, "What did I tell you?" to anybody who would listen.

"Damned old fool!" said the driver of the Clumber. "Just what we want at this minute, some idiot shoving himself under the wheels. One thing, he didn't get the number, and probably wouldn't know what to do with it if he had."

"I wouldn't be too sure," returned his companion gloomily. "Lots of idiots milling about on that crossing. Y'know, this job's been unlucky from the word go. Almost makes you think about going straight."

Eight

The clock was striking eleven as Miss Hiscock came back from market, sturdily pushing her market cart in front of her. Nearing her own house she was outraged to see a uniformed policeman on the step.

"The nasty thing!" she ejaculated. "At least the other had the decency to come in plain clothes. What will people think?"

Not that she needed to ask. She knew. They'd think the worst. She bumped the basket up the steps. The policeman turned.

"Miss Hiscock?"

"Who else?" She rootled in an enormous plastic bag for her latchkey. "I don't know why you're here, I'm sure."

"I'm enquiring for a Miss Janice Grey . . ."

"And I've told you already I don't know anything about a Miss Grey. The only girl who came in here for a room last Friday was called Jane Graham. And seeing she went down to the station last night to clear things up, I can't think why . . ." She found the key, pushed it into the lock and opened the door as if she had a grudge against it.

"I don't get it," said the constable. "What station was this?"

"The local one, of course. Where your chap came from."

She pulled him into the house and shut the front door.

"One of us is nuts," said the constable bluntly. "There's

no record of anyone coming down to the station in connection with this affair. I've only just left it."

"Come in and sit down," said Miss Hiscock, leading the way down the corridor. "I can't stand policemen eight feet tall glaring down at me. Now then, let's get things straight. One of your plain-clothes men came here yesterday asking about a girl who might have booked a room on Friday night, and when I told him about Miss Graham he said he'd be around again this morning. Then she came in—the girl, I mean—and she's got herself a job in the films somewhere, she's moving out today. She came down to the station last night after dinner, and when she got back she said everything was cleared up. Fixed was the word she used."

"That's what she said," the constable agreed. "Only—she didn't come."

Miss Hiscock looked grim. "She shouldn't have deceived me," she said. "Mind you, I couldn't blame her not wanting to get mixed up in something that's nothing to do with her, not with this job she's starting."

"I think I'd better see the young lady," suggested the visitor.

"I don't know that she's still here. I told you she was moving on today, and don't ask me for her address because she didn't give it and I didn't ask."

She looked longingly at the teakettle, she always made a cup first thing when she got back from the market, but she could see the officer meant business, so she went dispiritedly upstairs. The policeman came after her.

"She's not going to jump out of the window if that's what you think," snapped Miss Hiscock, but he kept on coming. The landlady tapped on the door, waited, called "Miss Graham," then turned the handle. The room wasn't only empty, it looked as though it had never been occupied. The bedclothes were folded, the window wide open. Miss Hiscock rushed across and shut that with a bang.

"That's a silly thing to do," she scolded no one in particular. "All the smuts . . ."

She looked around for a note, she couldn't believe the girl

had walked out without saying a word, then she reflected that most likely she'd hung about and, not knowing what time her landlady would return, had taken herself off.

"She'll probably write," she said, without much conviction.

"Why?" asked the policeman woodenly. "I mean, she didn't owe you anything, did she?"

"Rent's paid up for the week, if you want to know."

"And you didn't know her? I mean, you never saw her before Friday night?"

"What is all this?" demanded Miss Hiscock. "A Court of Enquiry? It just occurred to me that, as I was out when she left—that is, if she isn't coming back and I don't suppose she is—she might send a line or telephone this evening. She was a nice girl."

"But not above pretending she'd come to see us when she hadn't. Why did she say she'd come, anyway?"

"I told you, because one of your men was around here yesterday, asking questions. He said he'd be back this morning, so she said . . ."

"She'd come along to the station and clear everything up, only—she didn't come. And I'll tell you something else. Whoever that chap was who was calling here yesterday, he's got no right to wear a uniform on or off duty."

"You mean, he wasn't a policeman at all?"

"I mean just that."

"Then who on earth could he have been?"

"Someone else interested in Miss Grey's whereabouts, I suppose."

"She's not Miss Grey. Her name's Jane Graham. You can see the book for yourself."

"Did she offer any proofs of her identity?"

"I wouldn't dream of asking for them. Even with rooms as scarce in London as they are just now I'd soon have plenty vacant if I wanted everyone to prove he was who he said he was. I didn't ask you to prove your identity when you arrived, did I?"

"I can show you my warrant."

"Don't trouble yourself," retorted Miss Hiscock. "I wouldn't know if it was right or not. If they look respectable and have the money for the week, they're in."

"Did she say anything about her job?"

"She said she was an actress. Well, they don't always use their own names, do they? You don't mean she could *be* Janice Grey?"

"I don't know why else she should bolt when she hears the police are enquiring for her. No address left, I take it."

"The poor girl!" whispered Miss Hiscock. "With the both of you after her. What's the other lot want with her? Or don't you know?"

"Look," said the policeman patiently, "a man's been murdered, knocked on the head and hoved out of a train. He started the journey in the company of his wife, who was passing as Janice Grey. At the end of the journey Janice Grey vanishes. We want to trace her—for her own sake as much as anyone else's—if she only knew it, she probably needs protection."

"She knows it all right. You still didn't say who that other man might be, the one who didn't come from the police station."

"Someone else who was interested in Miss Grey's whereabouts. Might have been smarter to wait for us. Now, think. Did she ever mention anyone, any friend, any name at all?"

Miss Hiscock shook her head. Some women would have been thrilled to bits at the thought of becoming involved in what might turn into a *cause célèbre,* but not Emma Hiscock. All she asked was to be left alone, particularly by the police. The constable was pushing on, like an old horse turning a water wheel. "No telephone calls? No cards? Nothing?"

"I'll tell you one thing," Miss Hiscock remembered suddenly. "She used to go down to the Corner Café for her breakfast. Mind you, I don't see that it'll help . . ."

"Can't afford to disregard anything," said the man briskly. "Just on the cards she mentioned where this film was being made. Always assuming there ever was any film."

"I only know what she chose to tell me," said Miss Hiscock. "I let rooms, I'm not supposed to have second sight."

"If she should ring up or write, it will be your duty to contact us," the policeman informed her.

Miss Hiscock suddenly lost her temper. "Don't you start telling me my duty, young man," she stormed. "I've forgotten more about duty than you're ever likely to know. You stick to your own job, which is to find whoever killed that man who fell out of a train. And I'll never believe a little thing like that had the strength. But there's a man for you, put the blame on the first woman you see."

"I once had an aunt who kept a Kilkenny cat as a pet," the constable confided to a colleague later in the day. "Don't ask me why, set on being a martyr, I suppose. Well, this Miss Hiscock made me think of that cat. That's all."

He had left her house in a very thoughtful frame of mind. It seemed clear that the gang had been on the same lay as the authorities, trying to find the girl, and the gang had got there first. When they meet in the middle, O God save the Queen, he thought gloomily. Only before they reached the middle this other chap had jumped the gun.

The inspector wasn't going to like this, not one little bit.

Hoping to net a minnow if he couldn't bring home a whale, Perkins called at the Corner Café en route for the police station. The morning tea drinkers had gone, only one or two casuals dotted the little tables. Sally, who seemed to have solved the problem of perpetual motion, was moving with a machine-like speed that never appeared to affect her composure.

"What'll it be?" she asked, and that was the second time that day he felt he wasn't a welcome visitor.

"Actually, I'd like some information about one of your customers." And oh, the look she gave him! If he got back with both eyes where they'd been this morning he was going to be lucky.

"What are you trying to do?" inquired Sally. "Get my place shut down? Anyway, I don't have any information."

"There's a young lady been coming here for breakfast this past week, an actress she calls herself."

"Then I suppose that's what she is."

"Did she come in this morning?"

"What is all this?" asked Sally. "You must know she came in and if you have to arrest people I'd be obliged if you wouldn't do it on my premises. Place was nearly full at the time."

The policeman was silent for so long that she actually stopped working.

"Well, he was one of your lot, wasn't he? Here, what is it? Cat got your tongue?"

Still he said nothing, and her face changed with ludicrous speed.

"You don't mean he wasn't one of your lot?"

In reply, he asked another question. "What made you think he was a policeman?"

"Well. He went over to her table and started talking, and he put his hand in his pocket as if he was going to show her a warrant, but she stopped him. And then presently they got up and went out."

"And that's all you've got to go on?"

"Well, she was all worked up about this job, it's not likely she'd just have gone off with anyone who asked her. I mean, she just had this job, she was telling me. One thing I can tell you, she didn't know the fellow. And now I come to think of it he was quite a while making up his mind he knew her. So he couldn't have been her husband, say."

"No," agreed P. C. Perkins, "we don't think he was her husband, either. Are you telling me she just picked up her case and walked out with him without a word?"

"He carried the case and he fetched her a cup of coffee first. Quite the gentleman. Asked if she took sugar and all. Then they sat talking for a few minutes while she drank the coffee, and when she'd finished they just went out. Do you mean he came from the film studio, then?"

"I don't know anything about any film studio," countered Perkins, stolid as a teetotaler's Christmas pudding. "Happen to notice if they got into a car?"

"I wouldn't have seen it if they had, and if I'd had eyes

in the back of my head, which I have not. This is a no parking street, and I suppose even a police car 'ud have to wait round the corner."

She slammed a cup of tea on the counter in front of him. "Drink that," she hissed. "No need for all my customers to know you're here professionally."

"What I don't get," acknowledged Perkins, obediently sipping the tea, "is why you should be so certain he was the police, unless she'd dropped a hint that they were after her."

"I'm here to serve customers, not write film scripts," said Sally in crisp tones. "For all I know, everyone who drops in has got the police on their tail. No, it was her look partly, sort of—stricken. And I'll tell you this," she added, "everyone else thought he was the police, too. There was a bunch of cleaners in, come here every morning . . ."

P. C. Perkins set the plastic cup down on its indestructible saucer.

"Any idea where this new job of hers is? Or even if it exists?"

Two truck drivers looked in, saw the policeman and grinned.

"You been sanding the sugar, Sally?"

"Gentleman's had a shock," said Sally primly. These were old customers, she didn't have to ask what they wanted, cups of tea and immense buttered buns. When they had removed themselves to a table, with mock shivers because the law might be on their tail, too—there's no telling—Sally turned back to the policeman and answered his double question. Both her answers were in the negative.

She repeated the assurance she'd given him twice already. "I serve behind the counter, I'm not the *Daily News*."

The policeman tried again. "Would you know him again, do you think? Was there anything particular about him?"

"They come in in their baker's dozens," said Sally with marked patience. "They ask for a cup of tea or coffee or a packet of crackers. Half the time I don't so much as see them, and as for knowing one of them again, unless he had three eyes or a nose where a mouth looks to be, they wouldn't attract attention. I've told you, he looked pretty ordinary, not so tall as you, quietly dressed—not a van driver or anything like that, collar and tie, I do recall that—I took him for a plain-clothes copper."

He saw he would make no headway here and went back to the station to make his report.

"Might see if any of those cleaners noticed him in particular," suggested Inspector Frost, "though if they're the usual run they wouldn't notice anyone else if he came in naked. Full of their own affairs . . ." He sighed. Gilbert had declared that a policeman's lot is not a happy one, and how right he was.

The authorities were not alone in their justifiable anxiety about the whereabouts of Janice Grey, though their motives might be a little different. After the constable had left her house—and she couldn't have been more pleased to see a snake wriggle under the door—Miss Hiscock went back to the empty room and began vigorously to prepare it for its next occupant. The girl had a right to turn up any time after midday and Miss Hiscock wasn't of those who think it doesn't matter much, rooms being in such short supply, if everything isn't just as it should be. Besides, energy isn't only a good safety valve for emotion; in her case it always set her brain working double-quick time. Sweeping away like mad, letting the dust know where it got off, she was surprised to realize how much responsibility she felt for the missing girl. If she really was Janice Grey she'd had a pretty tough time, tougher than most wives, Miss Hiscock meant, and though, of course, it was wrong of her to land someone else in her dish of soup, it was unpleasant to think of her being run like a fox with the twin packs of the police and her late husband's criminal associates on her heels.

"Why, she hasn't got anyone," discovered Miss Hiscock, rubbing up the furniture till the surfaces glowed with discomfort.

And then she found it. It must have floated down from the mantelpiece behind the nest of drawers—a visiting card rather larger than normal and certainly less sedate. "Arthur Crook, Legal Adviser," she read, and "Your Trouble Our Opportunity." Sounds like a TV commercial, she thought, but drowning men clutch at straws and straws break camels' backs. Her head awhirl she went downstairs to make the long-awaited cup of tea.

Over it she concocted her plans. She would herself contact this Arthur Crook. Not by telephone, oh dear no. That way you simply got a smarmy secretary who said Mr. Crook was very heavily engaged for the next two weeks but he might be able to fit you in the week after that, by which time even the echo of the funeral hymns for the missing girl would have died away. If you want a thing done, do it yourself, and if you want to snare your bird don't give it warning you're coming. She looked impatiently at the kitchen clock. She supposed she must wait till midday and see this tiresome girl settled, and by that time the lawyer would be at lunch, but directly after lunch she would beard him in his den. She was as fond of clichés as Crook himself. So she set to, preparing the Irish stew for the lodgers' dinner, and she got into her Sunday costume and waited. The clock struck twelve and the girl didn't come—no sense of punctuality, grumbled Miss Hiscock—and then it was half-past and she got herself some bread and cheese, and after an eternity it was two o'clock and still no sign of the new lodger. Miss Hiscock said something to herself that Crook would have understood but a lady wouldn't, put on her hat and departed. From a local call box, two minutes from the office in Bloomsbury Street, she telephoned the number on the visiting card. She was prepared to tell off any smarmy secretary, but she had a jolt when Crook answered his own phone. Made her wonder if he was one of the tip-top lot. High-ups in her experience were never so readily available.

"Jane Graham?" said the booming voice at the other end of the line. "She's been pulling your leg, sugar. I never heard tell of the lady."

"She's got one of your cards, anyway. I found it in her room."

Light burst in the Bloomsbury office. "Didn't come off the Devon train last Friday night, I suppose?"

"That's just what she did, and the police have got some idea she might be this Janice Grey they're after. She . . ."

"Save it, sugar," said Crook's voice, booming like a sea in a storm. "Where are you speaking from? That's good. I'll expect you in a couple of minutes. As high as you can climb, but the welcome 'ull be all the warmer."

She was left in the telephone box with the receiver still at her ear. She felt a bit doubtful. Lawyers were never like this. She even wondered if there might be some link-up with the white-slave traffic. Still, if that was the fact, this Crook was going to get a nasty shock.

But when she had climbed the stairs at 123 Bloomsbury Street the shock was hers. A shabby office door was flung wide to welcome her.

"Come right in," exclaimed something that looked like a red grizzly bear. "I knew this was going to be my lucky day. I told Bill so, didn't I, Bill? There was a spider as big as my fist in my bath this morning, and that always means something good. Now sit down, you're looking a bit peaky, sugar, probably took those stairs too fast. A little refreshment . . ."

She didn't know how it happened, but there she was, sitting in a madly uncomfortable chair, with Crook beaming away on the other side of the table, and a glass of something pale gold in her hand.

"I'm a teetotaler," she tried to say.

"You show me the beer these days that isn't," Crook remarked. "Anyway, take it as medicine. Now, you've got some information about Miss Janice Grey."

"I don't know. She said her name was Jane Graham."

"Suppose you tell me what you do know and leave me to sort it out."

So she told him. "Like a bird flying through a tent," she said poetically. "Just in and out and now somewhere in the dark."

"You know," said Crook reflectively, "it's going to be a

rum set-up, me and the police on the same side. They ain't going to like it one little bit. But there, by the time we all get what we like we'll be fit for heaven."

"I'll never believe she pushed him out of the window," said the dauntless spinster in tones to which Crook had long become accustomed from women of her age and situation. "Only, if it turns out she did, then he asked for it, and she's not to blame."

"That's the spirit," approved Crook. "All the same, she's got a bit of explaining to do. According to her, X was doing the shoving. And we know X can't have been the husband because by the time I came upon her in a state of comparative suspension, Pat Wylie was already in his grassy bed. The train had passed the Falcon Estate, I remember noticing it through the window."

"Surely that shows that whoever tried to push her out had already disposed of the husband. Even a policeman must see that."

"Well, I see it and you see it, but the police are different. They insist on proof, proof that there ever was a third party, I mean."

"But she couldn't have pushed herself out of the door."

"She timed it very nice if she did," Crook agreed. "She didn't fall to her death, remember."

"I am thankful I found that card," said Miss Hiscock simply. "Mr. Crook, do you think this gang have got her?"

"That's one of the things it shouldn't be too hard to find out," Crook reassured her. "Keep in touch, sugar, if there should be any developments your end, and I'll let you know how my cookie crumbles."

He insisted on sending her back in a taxi, saying that whoever paid his bill—and I never pay my own, he told her, even if the chap who settles don't realize what he's doing—would account for that also. Then he went along to the police station. Not that they'd be able to tell him anything, he knew that, and of course he was right.

When he saw Crook come storming in, the duty sergeant let out a groan. The lawyer might believe his name began with the third letter of the alphabet, but the force knew it was really T for Trouble.

As he had anticipated, they didn't advance his knowledge a step. But just as he was turning to go, an angry young man barged in and went thundering up to the desk, demanding information about Janice's whereabouts.

"Are you a relation?" inquired the duty sergeant.

"No. My name is Frank James," he said. "I'm the one who's going to marry her if your chaps can restore her in one piece."

A huge hand clamped on his shoulder and he felt himself being guided toward the entrance.

"Don't you know better than to talk to the police like that?" boomed a voice like a foghorn.

Frank James twisted himself free to find an immense red face glaring into his.

"Who are you?" he demanded. His blood was up to such an extent it looked as though it would come to a boil at any moment. "Assistant Commissioner or something?"

Crook let out a roar that nearly deflected a passing bus and caused a baby in its carriage on the sidewalk to start to bawl.

"Tell 'em that at the Yard and watch their faces go red. Not that they ain't all the colors of a mandrill's behind as it is. Letting those thugs jump the gun . . ." He looked at his watch. "Too bad the pubs aren't open now, I could do with a pint. Now, you listen to your Uncle Arthur. I can see you haven't had much experience of murder. If you had, you wouldn't go bursting into a police station and spread the glad news that you're proposing to marry the girl."

"I am," insisted Frank sturdily.

"How long have you been of that mind?"

"Ever since I met her."

"See what I mean? When you met her she was a married woman, so if you wanted to put your plan through she had to become a widow. And now conveniently she is a widow. See my point about keeping your lip buttoned when you're talking to the authorities?"

"But, look here, I was in The Barley-Mow when she vanished," Frank protested.

Crook shook his big red head. "You underestimate the police, really you do, if you suppose they'd let a little thing like that stand in their way. Still, it's an ill wind and all that. Now how are you fixed for time? I don't mean just this minute, but next three days, say? Because if we don't find your girl within that time, I wouldn't give that for her chance." He held up a big finger and thumb in an irregular o.

"I can work it," said Frank recklessly.

"Good," said Crook. "Wouldn't surprise me if you and me were to work together fine. You see, it's quite likely we're goin' to need a stool pigeon, to hang around and ask questions and so forth. No good Bill or me—Bill's Bill Parsons, my A.D.C.," he added in an explanatory bracket—"taking on the job because if we tried to hide our lights under bushels the darn things would go up in sparks. But you," he regarded his companion affectionately, "you might be anyone."

"I suppose so," agreed Frank, without much enthusiasm.

"What you have to bear in mind is that these chaps are candidates for the high jump in any case, so one more name on their list of victims ain't going to bother them none."

"Actually, that had occurred to me," Frank told him.

"Try and see the police's point," Crook urged. "To them she's just the wife, widow rather, of a chap who's succeeded in making a lot of trouble for them. She knew they were responsible for at least one murder, and she lay low. Now they want to question her when said chap departs this life somewhat unconventionally, and she's still under cover."

"That's not her fault."

"That's what you think. But you ain't in their shoes. Come to that, you ain't even in mine."

"How do you come into this?" Frank interrupted.

Crook gave a gusty sigh, and then told him about the journey on Friday night and Miss Hiscock's visit that afternoon.

"Might almost say it's providence, mightn't you?" he wound up. "Anyway, that's what Miss H. is saying. You have to admit Sugar could have saved everyone, includin' herself, a lot of trouble by coming forward at the outset. She's got a bundle of info the authorities want, and you know the one about it bein' every citizen's duty . . ."

"Good grief!" exclaimed Frank. "You sound like Miss Malpas. You can't really believe those hoods would have let her get as far as a police station?"

"They didn't stop her gettin' latched onto Miss Hiscock. And there's a phone there, because she's given me the number. If she'd thought it too dangerous for the mountain to go to Mahomet, Mahomet would have buckled on its snowshoes and gone to the mountain. You can disagree with the cops all you please—it's practically my lifework—but you can't blame 'em for being suspicious of the lady's motives."

"Now if the gang know the police are onto them, as I suppose they do, what do you give for Jan's chances?"

"All depends on whether she's had the sense to keep her mouth shut or if she's blurted out that Crook's her friend. One consoling thought—it's a lot harder than the amateurs will ever believe to get rid of a corpse without attractin' attention. You can't go decorating the railway line from Paddington to Penzance."

"And, of course, she'll be a hostage."

Crook stared. "What for? Even the gang will know you can't strike bargains with the police."

The late editions were on the streets by this time and Crook stopped and bought one. Janice didn't make the headlines this afternoon, though you could be dead sure she would tomorrow—some enterprising journalist would have winkled the story out. The Prime Minister was meeting someone or other in Paris, a cat was mothering a canary and some idiot woman had had her car stolen. It was a white Clumber, No. ARP 1951.

It didn't mean a thing to Crook, not a thing.

"Where you putting up?" he asked his companion, folding the paper and sticking it into his overcoat pocket.

Frank said something vague about finding a place somewhere.

"Not been in London for some time, have you?" suggested Crook cheerfully. "Here, there's an empty telephone booth, probably the last you'll see for a week. Belt on and secure it."

When he joined the young man he yanked the receiver off its hook and telephoned to Miss Hiscock.

Miss Hiscock was trembling with outrage. "Would you believe it," she said, "that girl never came after all?"

"Maybe she came while you were with me."

"She could wait, couldn't she? Or leave a note in the letter box, like a Christian? No sense her coming now, I shall tell her the room's engaged, if she does."

"And you won't be telling her no lie," approved Crook. "I've got a lodger for you, young fellow called James. Young Lochinvar to you," he added explanatorily, "and just out of the West at that. Friend of our Miss Grey. Now, sugar, don't split my eardrum. I thought you wanted to be in on this. He's coming along right away as soon as he's collected his traps from the station."

"I've only got an overnight bag," said Frank.

"Oh well, ain't this the night the shops stay open late? Anyway, she won't know if you're sleeping in pajamas or your day shirt. She's a nice woman. It has its points."

"I suppose I ought to send my employers a wire," Frank reflected aloud.

"You do that," said Crook, "and if all goes well maybe they'll give you another week's leave for the honeymoon."

Nine

The police had, of course, been all over the ground, but that didn't deter Crook from emulating Good King Wenceslas' page. He wandered down to the café where he bought a cup of tea and stood at the counter manfully sipping it.

"New here, aren't you?" said Sally. "I mean, I haven't seen you before."

"So you do sometimes remember a face?"

"Depends on the face. What is it you want?"

She couldn't tell him any more than she had told the police. He showed her a picture of the girl that he had filched from Frank James—a picnic snapshot—and she said at once, "That's her. What's her name?"

And he said, "As if you didn't know. That's Janice Wylie, nee Grey."

Coming out he looked thoughtfully up and down the road. The café stood in a short line of shops running down to the High Street. He examined them. Hairdresser, dry goods, shoe repairer, dairy on one side; florist, arts and crafts disguised as an antique shop, druggist on the other. No stationer, he noticed, and recalled something Sally had said. "She didn't look any different that morning, except that she was carrying a case and had her newspaper under her arm and nearly lost it."

He popped back into the café. "Where do people hereabouts buy their papers?"

"There's an old chap on the corner, up those three steps by the church, he sells the morning papers. In the evening they pick them up at the station, there's no call for a man here. Those that have them delivered get them from Linnett's in Duke's Lane or Jones of the High Street."

"Know anything about the old chap?"

"Just that he sells papers. He's a widower, gets his pension and doesn't want to earn too much or they'll take it back again. Be all right this time next year, he'll be seventy and can earn what he likes. Drops in here on his way up."

"What time's that?"

"Six o'clock."

"What's your union thinking of, letting you work these hours?"

"So long as there are chaps on the road at 6:00 A.M. my place'll be open," she told him sturdily. "Very quiet at night, though. This girl got her papers from Tom, she passed the remark."

There being nothing more to do that night Crook went back to Bloomsbury Street, where a new client awaited him, another man who believed that money'll buy anything, including Crook's services. This was one of the times that he was disappointed.

"Think I want to find myself in jug for aiding and abetting?" he demanded, and if there had been any policeman within hearing he'd have fainted dead away. "I ain't fussy and my reputation can stand up to a lot, but even I have my limits."

The next morning he was up as early as Sally or Old Tom. And he joined them both in the café. Old Tom had just collected his papers.

"I see that woman's car's been brought back," he said in companionable tones, as he and Crook left the café together. "Must be crazy to go nicking a Clumber. They stick out a mile. It's a funny thing," he went on, unstringing his great bundle of papers, "you don't see a lot of them, not like Jaguars or these old Rollses, but I did see one yesterday morning, waiting in the lane there. White, too. Just a coincidence, of course."

"And just a coincidence you didn't notice the number?"

"Well, of course I didn't notice," said Tom. His first customer came up at this moment and the old man didn't have to ask him what he wanted. He just put a *Record* into the outstretched hand. "Still, like I say, just a coincidence."

Crook bought the loudest tabloid he could see and shook it open. MISS DINA PLANTAGENET'S CAR RETURNED. "Wonder what she was born," he said aloud. "Dinah Poops? Didn't happen to notice who was driving, I suppose?" he added.

"Two chaps were in it when it arrived," answered Tom. "The time? Oh, 7:45, say. It parked opposite the Cock Tavern and I thought, Well, you won't be able to stop there long. It's the day the tavern takes in its supplies, and they have to come early because, believe it or not, that lane's a two-way street for traffic. Half the time the cars drive on the sidewalk. One of these days they'll drive into a shopfront and then there will be trouble. One chap got out," he went on. "Didn't notice where he went, of course, no affair of mine."

"Didn't notice when he came back either, I suppose?"

Old Tom shook his head. "I did notice he wasn't there when the beer cart came up, and that was 8:15. Why, it wasn't mixed up in a jewel robbery, was it? I didn't read anything. . . ."

"Well," said Crook sensibly, "like you said, most likely he didn't have anything to do with Miss Dina Plantagenet."

He moved off. Of course, he was reflecting, they'd have to take Jan in a car, or she'd fuss like nobody's business when she realized they weren't going to no police station. They'd want everything nice and quiet—quiet as the grave. It was an unfortunate simile and he shied away from it at once. All the same, would they use a Clumber? As Old Tom said, they were pretty noticeable cars; but that might be a reason. No one would suspect it was stolen. He looked at the paper to see where it had been found. Apparently it had been returned to a street adjacent to Miss Plantagenet's bijou house in Belgravia.

"Mews apartment in Pimlico," he decided. "Wonder what time she reported it."

Because he had no idea how much Janice had confided in her captors and because he believed, without any feeling of conceit, that if he was out of the picture her chances were halved at the most generous estimate, he decided this was the moment to call on his stool pigeon. He rang Miss Hiscock's house. It was Frank who answered.

"You must have slept in your shirt," approved Crook. "Ever done any reporting jobs? Well, never mind. You must have seen 'Zero Hour Midnight' or whatever that program's called. You're going round to see Miss Dina Plantagenet, you represent the *Record* and they're interested in the story of the stolen car. Find out all you can about it, when it was taken, when it was brought back, when she telephoned the police."

"Do you think it could be the one Janice was taken off in?"

"If I knew that I wouldn't be on the phone," said Crook. "Don't mention the girl and use your loaf."

It was obvious from the exterior of her home that Miss Plantagenet had an artistic urge. The house was small—not to say poky—one of a short row in that part of Westminster that house agents promise you will shortly be as fashionable as other hitherto unfashionable parts of the city. Flowerpots, hung in wire baskets, decorated the basement; an immense cage of colored birds could be seen through the lowest window; heavy curtains must have shut out most of the light, for the rooms were small. The Clumber looked oddly out of place here, it had a kind of well-bred indifference to the effect it might produce. Miss Plantagenet's name was not a byword; she had done a little acting, a little radio work, a little television, but certainly not enough to justify the tenancy of this doll's house or the ownership of the car. Someone's little friend, thought Frank. Dina herself answered the door, after an impressive pause, wearing very trim slacks and an immense roll-collared sweater; she had hair that was almost lint-white and as smooth as silk; she wasn't quite so young as her publicity agent made her out to be, but Frank could quite realize that someone whose tastes turned that way might think her worth the rent of the house.

"Oh, not again," she said when she saw Frank. "I've nothing to add. If I'd known there would be all this fuss I'd never have reported the loss of the car at all, especially as it was brought back within twenty-four hours."

"You haven't told *me*," said Frank with his most engaging smile. "And I'm not the police, if that's what you're thinking. Press," he added in a voice that he tried to make sound both casual and important. "The *Record*."

She was less impressed than he had hoped. "Why did you come? There's nothing particular about my case."

"Except the car," said Frank quickly and lovingly.

She laughed suddenly. "Have you come to do a commercial about the car? Tell me, how long have you been a reporter?"

"Not long," he confessed. "That's why it's important I shouldn't make a botch of this."

"So that's my market value. The latest recruit. Did you bring a photographer with you or do you take your own pictures?"

"They wouldn't give me a photographer," said Frank, recovering rapidly. "Of course, they have got a great many photographs."

"Haven't you even got a weeny box camera?" She came down the steps and posed beside the car, leaning one arm on the dusty white hood. "Well, go ahead. What do you want me to tell you?"

"What did you feel like when you found the car had gone?"

"I thought this was a chance for the police to do their stuff, so I rang them up. Mind you, I knew there were only two kinds of chaps who'd make off with a Clumber, a man who wanted to impress his girl or someone doing a smash-and-grab, looking for something that starts without a sound and goes faster than light."

"Wouldn't a Clumber be a bit conspicuous for a crime?"

"That's the reason. I say, don't you have to take notes of

all this, or is it true what they say, that you've written the interview before you ring my bell?"

"You mean, the police wouldn't suspect a Clumber because it would be running an unnecessary risk? Which do you think it was?"

"Well, there's nothing in the paper about a smash-and-grab. Anyway, I know it was a girl, the car came back reeking of scent. I've had to have the windows open. . . ."

"It does seem rather an odd time of day to take a car for joy-riding," Frank ventured.

"Odd? Why, what time of day do you suppose it was taken? It was taken at night, of course. Even a teenager would hardly dare remove a Clumber in broad daylight. Even if I was at work or indoors someone would see it and think it a bit queer. No, I didn't discover the loss till the morning, when I was brought down by the postman, because as it happened I had an early night for once, and I don't have a cat to put out or a dog to take walkies, so while I watched crime on television the real thing was going on outside."

Frank walked around and inspected a nasty mark on the car's offside door.

"That hasn't done it any good," he observed candidly.

"A driver with one arm round his girl and about half an eye on the road is likely to come to grief," retorted Dina. "I've been onto the insurance about it."

"Where actually was it found?"

"There's a kind of lovers' lane near the old church that was bombed in the war and has never been rebuilt. You'd be surprised how many quite serviceable cars park there of an evening—or again, perhaps you wouldn't. Anyway, that's where she was left. Someone rang me up and said she was there and they were quite right. There she was. Might even have been the chap who took her, but it wasn't, of course. It was a policeman. I'm afraid it's not much of a story for you," she went on. "But I daresay you'll be able to make something romantic out of it."

Suddenly she turned her head, she assumed a listening attitude.

"Do you hear a telephone?"

He listened. "Yes. But I don't think it's yours. It sounds too far off."

"Mine's upstairs. It seemed such a good idea to have it in my bedroom, then I could lie down and chat whenever I had a mind. I'd forgotten how often I should have to do the stairs when I happened not to be in bed." She moved up the steps. "You won't go?"

"Of course I won't."

As soon as the door had closed and he could hear her steps receding, he opened the car and released the two back doors. If Janice had been taken away in this, then she'd have been in the back seat, where she'd be less noticeable; she was a clever girl, she must have realized she wasn't being taken to the station, surely she'd try and leave some clue. Only what? And where? He tipped up cushions, shifted a rug, peered under the seat. When he found the clue he didn't believe it, it was too much like a fairy tale. Yet there it was in his hand, a scrap of linen, very plain with hand-drawn borders. There was no initial, no laundry mark, but he knew it must be hers because of that faint scent of Genêt Fleuri. He knew no one else who used that particular scent. He jumped out of the car just as Miss Plantagenet reappeared.

"Someone offering you a new part?" he said warmly. "The *Record's* always interested . . ."

Her voice would have frozen the phoenix.

"What's the idea?" she demanded. "Pretending to be a reporter and all that. Whoever put you up to that game must be dumb. I've been meeting reporters all my professional life. Anyone could tell at a glance you don't know the first thing about it. Well, come on, let's have a scrap of truth for a change."

"I assure you," he began, but she broke in. "You asked if that was someone offering me another part. Does it surprise you to know it was the *Record* asking if it would be convenient for their representative to come round and take a few photographs?"

"It would stagger me," replied Frank promptly. "Papers

don't ring up celebrities and ask if it's convenient to call. They know only too well they'd probably find the bolts drawn."

"Are you calling me a liar?" the girl demanded.

"I think someone's leading you up the garden path. In fact, you could do worse than ask for police protection."

"Oh yes, our police are so efficient, aren't they? They found my car, I suppose? Of course they didn't. And they wouldn't. What's one car more or less to them?"

"I'm not speaking without the book," Frank assured her. "If this chap should turn up, you want to watch your step. This car may have been used in connection with a crime."

"You think fast," she approved. "It's no crime to take a girl joy-riding, it isn't even a crime to borrow a car so long as you return it. As for watching my step, you're the one I should keep my eye on."

"Look," said Frank, "let me come in and use your phone. I'll ring up the *Record* and they'll confirm what I say."

He wouldn't do anything of the kind, of course, but she wouldn't know if he dialed Crook's number, and you could rely on Crook to play ball all around the clock. The chap gave you the impression he'd been born with four hands. Made his fortune as a juggler, if he hadn't preferred to make it in some other capacity.

"You must think *I'm* dumb," Miss Plantagenet scoffed. "If you're so anxious to get inside the house you should have borrowed a uniform and pretended to come to examine the gas."

"Too chancey," said Frank. "You might only use electricity. Look, are you there alone?"

She stared at him incredulously, and he stared back, solemn and eager.

"What do you think?"

"If there'd been anyone else you'd have let him answer the phone, so I suppose you are. Look, you must have heard about this girl who's missing."

"Probably holed up somewhere near by laughing like a drain at the publicity she's getting. Doesn't she call herself an actress, just up from the provinces?"

"The police are trying to hang a murder rap on her," said Frank, crisply. Too late he remembered Crook's warning.

Slowly her face changed. "You really are in earnest, aren't you? Is that why you're here?"

He snatched at caution like someone trying to catch the tail of an escaping cat.

"I told you, I represent the *Record.*"

"Oh, we're back at that, are we? Well, I've told you, I don't believe you, and if I did I wouldn't have any statement to make."

"Then you won't let this other chap in?"

"Why don't you hang around and have a word with him?"

He saw he was cutting no ice. She laughed and shrugged and went back to the house. But before she went she ostentatiously locked the car.

Frank walked away up the little street and found a telephone box. When he got Crook's office he learned that Crook himself was out.

"When's he likely to be back? Have you any idea?"

"Try in about an hour," Bill Parsons counseled him in that voice that always seemed to suggest that even the news that the bomb was about to be dropped wouldn't move him.

"I think I'm onto something," ventured Frank.

"See it doesn't get away from you," murmured Bill, and hung up.

"She knows something," Frank assured himself, leaving the box. "Did that phone really ring or was she going back for orders? Only, in that case, wouldn't there have been some effort to stop me getting away?"

He didn't for an instant believe the *Record* had telephoned, but very likely someone was coming along just to check up. No harm in doing a bit of sentry-go. His first shock, at the notion that Crook could take any interest in any other case, wore off. Anyway, Janice was his girl and it was up to him, etc., etc.

These amateurs, Crook used to marvel, rushing in where angels fear to tread. True, now and again they managed to put one over the angels, but it didn't happen often. Mostly they simply provided more business for the funeral director.

Frank's first step was the obvious one of looking up Miss Plantagenet's number in the book and ringing the house. If a man answered, he'd know some of his suspicions at least were justified. But though he could hear the bell pealing away, no one answered. He tried again a little later with the same result.

Mr. Proudie kept one of those numerous little shops labeled Antiques that, with restaurants and self-service stores, establish themselves wherever a TO LET notice goes up. Mr. Proudie was an elderly man rather like a walrus; he had great contempt for what he called the upstarts. His shop had been run by the same family for nearly 150 years, passing from father to son, but his only son had fallen in the war so he'd be the last of them. He was fidgeting about at the back, examining some bits of glass he'd bought at a sale when he noticed a chap poring over the contents of what he called the trash bucket on the sidewalk outside. His grandfather would have spun in his grave like a tee-to-tum to see the tricks you had to get up to now to attract custom. If you bought a lot at a sale you could be sure of finding several bits worth half a crown or less. Mr. Proudie had learned, like Crook, that there is a passion for obtaining a bargain, whether you need it or not, implanted in many a female breast, and he put all these bits and pieces on a butler's tray just outside the door. The shop was on a corner and it was surprising how many people did stop and finger the charming cup minus its saucer, the Staffordshire sheep with one ear missing, the pin box, the odd glass vase. Of course, there was no profit to speak of in this kind of sale, but the important thing was it brought them inside the shop, and in a day when a sixpenny-halfpenny Victorian ornament, a pig leaning over a stile or a mouse escaping from the toe of a white china slipper, would fetch a pound, and also with competition what it was, you couldn't afford to miss a trick. Mostly it was women who stopped, but this potential customer was a man, a chap with a peaked motoring cap pulled over his face and a checked scarf wrapped round his throat. On the wall of the shop hung a magnificent gilt looking glass complete with candelabra, and the chap kept staring at it. It had been hung at a cunning angle and reflected quite a lot of the little street, including, though Mr. Proudie didn't at the moment appreciate this, the door of No. 8 Spring Terrace where Miss Plantagenet lived. This fellow kept picking up bits and putting them down. Mr. Proudie, who was an expert at this sort of thing, became suspicious. Whatever the man wanted, it wasn't anything in the tray.

He came to the door. "See anything there that interests you?"

The man nodded toward the gilt-edged glass. He was younger than Proudie had suspected, and the old man decided he was up to no good.

"Eighty-five pounds," he said promptly, and launched into a history of the piece.

"Very interesting." The young man edged himself a few inches nearer. "No magical properties, I suppose."

"Is that intended for wit?"

"You must have heard of the famous looking glass that reflected the scenes it had stored up. You know, the girl looked into the glass like this"—he looked intently, but in No. 8 nothing stirred—"and another face appeared looking over her shoulder. And when she looked around, there was no one there."

"Too bad," said the old man, "this isn't the one."

"You wouldn't be selling it for eighty-five pounds if it were. Still, I daresay you do a good trade. Tenants who can afford to run Clumbers . . ."

"Don't come in here," retorted the old man promptly. "What's your game?"

It was practically what Dina had said.

"You get along," Proudie continued, "unless you want me to call a policeman."

"Here, wait a minute," said the young man firmly. "You may own this dump, but you don't own the sidewalk in front of it. Why, a chap hasn't even got the legal right to park his car in front of his own house."

"You've got cars on the brain," said the old man. "Well, I don't deal in cars, not any kind."

"Oh, I wouldn't say that." The young man's hand came out and he picked up a brooch—old Mr. Proudie dealt in everything these days. It represented a tiny car, what used to be called a horseless carriage. "Fancy driving around in that. Not that I'd scorn it if nothing better offered."

"Do you mind?" The old man came out and removed the bauble. "Now, sir, if you're interested in anything."

At that moment a policeman passed on his beat. The difficult customer asked, "What's the price of that china cat wearing a boater?"

"Two pounds," said the old man sullenly.

The policeman stopped. "Morning, Mr. Proudie." He looked meaningly at the young man.

"Robbery," said the young man. "Let's ask an independent witness. What 'ud you give for that cat, officer?"

"I wouldn't take it as a gift," said the officer promptly. "I wouldn't dare. I'm a married man and it 'ud be as much as my life was worth to take back something else for my wife to dust. Very neat, my wife is. Eat off the floor and all that."

"They ought to pay you more," said the young man sympathetically. "Then you could buy a table."

The policeman instantly took offense, but before he could speak the other had dodged into the doorway. The gilt glass had fulfilled its purpose at last. Someone was coming down the steps of No. 8. Whoever he was, he didn't represent the *Record*, the watcher decided. No notebook, no raincoat, certainly no camera. He turned purposefully in the direction away from the corner shop, a tall man in a light gray coat and a snapbrim hat pulled forward. He carried an umbrella over his arm.

"I'll try again another day," the young man promised, moving into the narrow residential street.

"What was all that in aid of?" demanded the constable.

"He's been hanging about this long while. I don't like it. There's something called casing the joint, and I live alone above the shop. I know this isn't Christie's, but there have been too many of these small break-ins, and it doesn't always stop at burglary. He had his eye on that glass. You mark my words, something 'ull come of this."

If Crook had been there he might have capped the quotation—his mind was a jumble of odd literary allusions, picked up heaven knows where. "Let's hope," he might have said, "it won't be human gore." And for good measure he could have added, "Hope is not yet taxed."

Ten

The man who came down the steps of No. 8 walked easily toward a telephone booth at the top of the narrow road, pulled open the door and stepped inside. Frank took off the checked scarf and put it in his pocket; though the day was chilly he felt a flame of warmth running through him. He forced himself not to hurry, sauntering along as though he had all day and nothing to do with it. When the man's back was turned toward him, slipping the coins into the box, Frank ran lightly up the steps of No. 8 and rang the bell. No one answered. He waited and rang again, but still no one came.

"Taking my advice to heart and not letting strangers in," he told himself.

Long net curtains were draped American-fashion across the windows, he couldn't see a thing. When the telephone box was empty he made his way toward it; it smelled of cigar smoke. He dialed her number but again there was no response and the anger rising in him as his conviction grew that this woman knew something about Janice, that to some extent even Janice's safety might lie in her hands, sent him boiling back to the doorstep. When no one answered he caught the handle and found that the tongue of the lock was not completely engaged. Obviously the door stuck and no one had bothered to plane it. The man who had gone out might have believed he had closed the door. He registered half consciously that the woman hadn't seen him off the premises. Someone she knew then. He pushed urgently against the lock and suddenly it gave and he was in the house, feeling like Alice when she fell through the hole and found everything smaller than life. The little house was quite dark, with low ceilings. All the doors were closed, but as his eyes became accustomed to the gloom he picked out a white telephone standing in a recess within reach of his hand. So that was lie number one nailed, he thought grimly. She'd said the phone was upstairs and she had made quite a thing of having to go up whenever the blessed thing tinkled. And it hadn't rung while they were talking, because she'd left the front door ajar and he couldn't have failed to hear the bell. He opened the door nearest him and saw a dim room furnished chiefly by a cocktail cabinet and an outsize television set. No pictures, no books, and no one there. The kitchen was no more than a box and that was all there was on that floor; he ran lightly up the stairs calling, "Anyone at home?" his heart beating like a drum at the thought of whom he might find. There were two more rooms upstairs, the first was empty like the sitting room, and when he tried the door of the other one it was locked. He hammered on the panels.

"Let me in." Then he stopped and put his ear against the keyhole but heard nothing. He discovered something, though. The key wasn't on the inside of the door, so it must have been locked from without. He was quite convinced he knew who was concealed there and began to call Janice's name, then suddenly stopped, feeling a fool for not realizing that it's possible to lock a room from the inside and withdraw the key. Only—why? he thought. Why?

He straightened and stood there a moment, still with that sense of being a size too large for the walls and doors about him. Then he lunged, shoulder to the panels. The house had been built for artisans or coachmen, he thought, and commanded a pretty price after World War II. Probably the job had been skimped since money was easy come by this way. The old doors had been removed, they'd have presented much more of a problem, being solid grained wood; the new ones were the usual hollow type. He felt this one give quickly under his battering. But before he got through, his heart was like a stone in his breast. Anyone living, he thought, must realize what was going on, would surely make some sign, utter some cry.

But they may have drugged her—she may be gagged. It occurred to him with a nasty sense of shock that they might even have put a watch on the house. Or possibly Dina Plantagenet was hidden somewhere, watching him—though where, if she wasn't actually behind the wallpaper, was anybody's guess. He remembered that the white car hadn't been driven away, but was still standing at the curb.

The door gave way and he fell into the room. His hand moved automatically toward the wall switch and in an instant the place was full of a golden light. He believed he had been prepared for any horror, but not for this, not for this. He moved, like someone drugged toward the divan with its chichi colored spread. Miss Plantagenet lay there, head propped foolishly against a satin-fringed cushion. A scatter cushion, he thought, not knowing he thought it; her hair fell limply over her cheek, her hand dropped toward the floor. She wasn't gagged, she wasn't drugged, he knew that at once.

"She's dead," he whispered. "She's dead."

He stood looking, paralyzed, while his brain whispered, "Get the police, go on, there's a telephone," and some drugged creature that was himself argued patiently back, "But don't you see, there's no sense, they can't do anything. She's dead."

It was the footsteps that brought him suddenly back to the present catastrophe. They sounded in the hall, and he stiffened, danger whistling in his ear like a siren. Somebody had been watching the house, after all. The girl who occupied the place hadn't been a dumb fool. She'd known he wasn't a reporter, that he'd come for some other reason. She'd told the man about her visitor. She had probably broken up Frank's conversation with her in order to telephone the man he had seen, to ask for instructions. Had she known he'd come back? The steps approached the stairs, he heard them shaking under that deliberate tread. He threw one anguished glance about him, as if in search of cover, but, of course, there was none. He drew back against the wall behind the broken door. The footsteps came on; the door that had swung half closed was pushed wider. Someone came in. At the same instant Frank extinguished the light and leapt; he felt the man stagger, then come crashing down. Frank leapt over the prone finger and made for the stairway. The house was still in darkness, except where a faint gray pencil of light came through the door leading to the street. Down the stairs he pelted, expecting every instant that the man he had felled would pull himself together and come swaying after him. As he reached the hall the sitting-room door swung wide and he felt himself enclosed in arms that might have belonged to a grizzly bear.

"Not so fast," called a voice, and he knew they had the last laugh, after all. While he struggled to get free, with no more chance than that poor girl upstairs had had in her fatal encounter, his other enemy grunted and got to his feet.

"Down here, Ted," said the man who held him captive, and then at last the light went on.

"No trouble, mind," his captor warned, but Frank was past fighting. Astonishment held him rigid. The man who had got him in that tigerish grip wore the blue uniform of a police sergeant and the man he'd jumped on and who was now coming to join them was, he could see, the same one he'd talked to near the antique shop. He couldn't imagine what they were doing here.

Recognition was mutual.

"He said you weren't up to no good," said the police officer.

"That old codger!" Frank dismissed him with a word. "Did you put on the light? Did you see her?"

"I saw 'er. I'd best get the station on the phone," he added. "Doctor—though there's not much he can do, fingerprints, the lot."

Suddenly he seemed to realize he was talking to his superior officer and he said apologetically, "Well, yes, I forgot, you don't know. There's a dead woman on the couch up there, and by the look of her I'd say she'd been murdered."

Something like a firework split in Frank's brain.

"They do train you to be observant in the Force," he cried.

"That'll do," said the man who held him. "I should keep anything you've got to say for the station. Ted, you get the station and explain and ask them to send a car. I wouldn't trust this bloke as far as I could throw him."

"I know the man you want," said Frank, less acclimatized to violence than either of his companions. "That is, I don't know his name, but he's round about six feet, wearing a gray overcoat and a dark hat and smoking a cigar."

"You'll be able to tell the inspector that."

"So I shall. But, of course, by that time he'll be wearing a blue coat and a brown hat and the cigar will have been finished."

The policeman thought he was like someone coming out of ether after an operation, didn't know what he was saying. Or else he was playing it smart. Ted was talking on the line, after a minute he came back and said everything was being laid on.

"I'll ask you to accompany us now," said the sergeant. "We shall want a statement. I expect you know your rights."

"I don't have to answer any questions without my lawyer being present." Frank glanced at the watch on his wrist. "I was due to telephone him about now in any case."

"You can do that from the station. Did you have a coat?"

"No," said Frank vaguely, "and if I had I'd still be wearing it. This isn't exactly a social call."

"Would this be yours, sir?" asked Ted, producing something from behind his back like the inevitable conjurer with the inevitable rabbit. He held out a brown-and-white checked scarf.

"That's right," Frank agreed. "I stuffed it in my pocket. Where was it?"

"On the floor in the lady's room, quite near the sofa actually."

"I suppose it fell out when I—when I bent over her. It's odd, I knew she was dead, but I couldn't believe it. We'd been talking such a short time before . . ."

"The best thing you can do is save that for later," the older policeman warned him. "You'll have plenty of chances to talk, more I daresay than you'll want to take. That car coming, Ted?"

"On its way."

"You better wait here. What's the number?" He took out a notebook and jotted down the telephone details.

"What made you come here?" asked Frank. "I mean, you don't usually go marching into private houses, do you?"

"It depends on whether anyone's broken into them first."

"The door wasn't locked," Frank murmured. "It didn't look broken into."

"We had word," said the policeman briefly.

"You mean, some good citizen—no, of course not." Light broke. "It was the chap in the phone box. He must have seen me come up the steps, saw me get inside perhaps and realized this was his chance. Call the police—did you ever hear the story of the cockroach and the tortoise?"

"Getting light-headed again," decided the policeman, "or giving us another waltz up the garden path."

"A cockroach knew it would be devoured by the tortoise, so it lodged itself in the one place where it couldn't be destroyed, under the tortoise's armpit. This chap knows he's killed a girl, so you'd argue, wouldn't you, he'd stay as far away from the police as he could. Then he sees someone else coming into the house and thinks, This is my chance. Don't you see that's how it must have happened?"

"We'll sort it all out," said the policeman. "You leave it to us."

Suddenly Frank was angry again. "You haven't got far in your hunt for Janice Grey," he taunted them. "Why should I suppose you'll be any sharper here?"

"So that's where you come in, is it?" Frank realized with a shock that this was the first time Janice's name had been mentioned. Since it rang in his own mind like an eternal bell, he could hardly conceal the amazement on his face. "What made you think Miss Plantagenet had anything to do with her?" the policeman asked.

Frank's lips folded over in a very prim expression. "As you've just reminded me, I don't have to answer any questions —until I've seen my lawyer. Mr. Crook . . ."

"So he's in for you, too?"

"You ought to close that telephone box at the end of the street," Frank told him excitedly. "That chap was ringing someone from there. I could smell his cigar when I went in a bit later. I couldn't get any answer when I rang the bell, you see, so I thought I'd try the phone. His fingerprints will be there, he might even have dropped the stub of his cigar."

"Car's here," said Ted stolidly. Frank might have been talking Choctaw for all the attention the police paid him.

Crook was back in his office when Frank rang for the second time. He listened for a moment, then hung up briskly.

"Who says our young men haven't got enterprise?" he inquired of Bill Parsons. "Mostly when a pressman pushes his way into a private house and there's a row, he's the one who's carted away on a stretcher, but in this case it's the lady of the house who's the corpse."

"She must have said something that annoyed him," murmured Bill in his indifferent way.

"And somehow the police have got the notion he's responsible," Crook continued. "Young Frank wants me to go down and sort it out for him."

At the station he found Frank in a state of considerable excitement and indignation, but in nowise apprehensive or dejected. Crook saw that his feeling was not for his own danger, in which at present he did not believe, but a conviction that he'd stumbled on a thread that might lead them, if not to Jerusalem's wall, at all events to the place where Janice was concealed.

His statement to the police was merely an enlargement of the answers he had given them on their arrival.

"I see, Mr. James," said the Inspector. "What I don't see is why you should have assumed that Miss Plantagenet had anything to do with Miss Grey's disappearance."

"It was her car," Frank explained.

"If we're going to suspect everyone whose car is stolen for the purpose of committing a crime . . ." the Inspector began.

"Anyway, that's why I went to see her. To find out if she knew anything about its being used to decoy Miss Grey."

"Did you suppose she'd tell you?"

"People often tell you things without realizing it," insisted Frank.

"And that's what she did?"

"I think she told me more than she knew. But that's not all. I found this handkerchief pushed down the side of the seat Miss Grey would have occupied, the one behind the driver."

"How can you be certain she was sitting there?"

"Oh come," protested Crook. "Because a chap's a murderer and a thug and runs a gang of hoodlums, he don't have to have the manners of a hog. If you're handling a lady into a car, well, she gets in first, don't she, which means she takes the further seat, and in a country where you drive on the left-hand side of the road that means she's sitting behind the driver. Any complaints?"

"This handkerchief, sir," said the Inspector, disdaining Crook's question. "You didn't mention this to the police."

"I didn't have much chance. And when I remembered it I decided to wait for my legal adviser."

The Inspector was examining the handkerchief.

"Is there any proof that this belonged to Miss Grey? It's not marked, there's no initial."

"It's the sort she always used. Anyhow, you can compare it with the others she had—the handkerchief, I mean."

"Be your age, Frank," Crook suggested. "They haven't located Miss Grey yet, let alone her luggage. Still, it all adds up, don't it? I mean, we know—at all events my client and me do—that a white Clumber with two gents in it drew up near the Corner Café not half an hour before Miss Grey vanished. No," he went on quickly, forestalling the Inspector's obvious question, "I don't know the number, it didn't occur to my informant it might be wanted, but some circumstantial evidence is pretty compulsive, as when you find a trout in the milk. What 'ud you like to bet that car never went further afield from Spring Terrace than Paddington?"

"We happen to know it went at least as far as Mill Hill," said the Inspector dryly. "It was involved in an incident at a pedestrian crossing, and though it failed to stop, a passer-by noted the number and gave it to a police constable, who reported the matter to us."

"Sounds like the house that Jack built, don't it?" was Crook's irreverent comment. "What time was this?"

"The morning in point."

"I meant the actual time."

"Is that so important?" snapped Frost.

"It could make all the difference between a life sentence and a ring of wedding bells," retorted Crook poetically. "Because I'd bet my Sunday-go-to-meeting hat that the car was reported stolen *after* its number had been taken by the boys in blue. Well, work it out for yourself," he urged, perceiving no mellowing in the rocky face before him. "Once the authorities have got the number they're going to track down the owner. And if said owner declares the car's been stolen, so she ain't responsible, it's going to look a bit rum that she didn't think of reporting it to the police. After all, this was a Clumber, not a bubble car. What I mean to say is the police are going to start scratching their woolly heads and wonder what's cooking." He turned to Frank. "Did she happen to mention when she noticed the car was missing?"

"When she came down that morning to open the door to the postman; she said she supposed it had been taken after dark the previous night."

"Shouldn't be too hard to find out what time the mail's delivered in those parts," Crook suggested. "Normal thing when a whacking great car like that vanishes is to notify the police right away, unless you've a pretty ripe idea who's got it. Well, there's one Clumber missing and there's another Clumber turning up outside the Cock Tavern shortly before eight o'clock. And there's a young lady missing and a handkerchief that could be hers is found in said Clumber, which we now know to be the property of the late Miss Plantagenet."

"That's speculation, Mr. Crook," said Frost in crisp tones. "Right now I want to get Mr. James's story. So far he's admitted calling on Miss Plantagenet and has shown us a handkerchief he says he took out of her car. Did Miss Plantagenet see you take it, sir?"

"She pretended to hear the telephone, which she said was in her bedroom and that's why it sounded so far away, but in fact the telephone's in the hall and it wasn't ringing. She was away for about a couple of minutes, time enough for me to examine the car and find the handkerchief, and when she came back the temperature had dropped about forty degrees."

"Although no one had telephoned her?"

"She could have done the telephoning herself. Say she became suspicious. Well, of course, she tumbled right away that I wasn't really a reporter. . . ."

"Probably took you for one of the C.I.D." said Crook maliciously. "Can't blame her trying to contact her boy friend if she did."

"She came back," insisted Frank, oblivious to the implied badinage between Crook and the authorities. "If she'd thought I represented danger to her—physical danger, I mean—why didn't she stay safely behind her front door?"

"Perhaps she wanted to know what you were up to," suggested the Inspector.

"Of course she did. She came back with a cock-and-bull story about the real reporter from the *Record* being on the line and when I offered to come in and telephone the office and let her hear the answer, she wouldn't have me over the threshold."

The Inspector's face spoke for him. Can you wonder at it? it said. Aloud he asked, "Why were you so anxious to get into the house?"

"I wanted to know who was in it besides herself."

"You mean you thought she might have Miss Grey hidden there?"

"She knew something about her that proved she had inside information, and then the car was left close by when it was returned. I had to know," he repeated passionately.

"What makes you so sure she had inside information?"

"She said Janice Grey was passing herself off as an actress. How did she know that? It never appeared in the press, and I had every paper that's published. She knew either because Jan had told her or because one of the gang had told her. There's no other way she could have known."

"He's right, you know," said Crook admiringly. "It wasn't in the papers. I know because Miss Hiscock told me—who told you?" he added.

"No one," said the Inspector, "not until we heard from the girl at the café that Miss Grey had got a job in the films."

"And that hasn't emerged in print?" cried Frank excitedly.

"All right. Miss Plantagenet knew Miss Grey was passing herself off as an actress. That made you certain she knew more than she should. Why didn't you come to the station and tell us what you'd learned?"

"I hadn't any proof she'd told me about Jan being an actress. I couldn't even prove I'd found the handkerchief in the car. Only I was convinced not only that she knew of my suspicions but that she'd passed that information on to someone else."

"How do you make that out, sir?"

"The woman's dead, isn't she?" suggested Crook.

"After I left, she had a visitor."

"You mean, you saw a third party enter the house. You didn't tell us that."

"I saw him leave—after she was dead. He couldn't have left if he hadn't originally gone in. So . . ."

"Take it easy, Frank," warned Crook. "Remember, you're dealing with a body that works on proof—not hunches like me or spec like you, or even common sense like most of the hoi polloi. Later on you're going to be telling this story in court, and then you'll be on oath, so you want to be careful. What the Inspector means is, did you see this chap go into the house?"

"No," Frank was bound to admit, "I didn't. But then I had to telephone your office and afterwards I went along to a men's outfitter and bought the cap and scarf. So there was plenty of time for someone to get there. And I daresay he was watching to make sure he wouldn't be seen."

"Speculation again," sighed Crook.

"Did you notice a car, besides the Clumber, of course, in front of the house when you returned?" asked the Inspector.

"No. Because there wasn't one."

"So he came on foot?"

"He certainly left on foot. I saw him. He went into the telephone booth at the top of the road, the one I'd used when I tried to get in touch with you," he added, turning to Crook.

"There are other residents in the street. Isn't it odd none of them saw him arrive?"

"Have you asked them?" demanded Frank.

"We've been making enquiries. So far no one's been found who saw him come."

"Don't tease him, Inspector," said Crook indulgently. "What he means, Frank, is that perhaps this chap didn't arrive after you left, maybe he was there already. I daresay when you were talking to the lady your eyes were mostly on the car. I thought as much. How can you be so tooting sure he wasn't behind a curtain somewhere giving her the wigwag, which would explain her suddenly hearing a phone and goin' in for instructions."

"Yes, of course. I hadn't thought." He looked eagerly at the Inspector and then faltered for the first time.

"You don't believe there ever was another man," he said. "I tell you, I saw him leaving the house. And someone rang you up. Did he give you a name? Why didn't he wait till you arrived?"

"He doesn't have to—give a name, I mean. If you'd been a policeman as long as I have, Mr. James, you'd realize how loath a proportion of the public is to be associated with us in public."

"I daresay they have their reasons," said Crook.

"I told you to test the telephone for fingerprints," cried Frank fiercely.

"A public phone box? You'd used it after this anonymous

caller, and I daresay several people since. The only fingerprints on Miss Plantagenet's phone are her own. There are others in the house, of course. We'll need to take yours for comparison. . . ."

"You have to remember," Crook put in, "you're dealing with a gang who think no more of taking a life than you or me would think of taking a bus ticket. This girl's let their side down, made it obvious she knows a bit too much, or so this chap believes. Anyway, there's a dust-up and she's left for the undertaker. And then providence hands you to them on a plate. You've been there in the morning and you turn up again in a disguise that wouldn't deceive a poodle dog, and you're actually on the premises when the police come in. After all, it must be obvious Miss Plantagenet didn't do that to herself, and you've been hanging around—did anyone see you?"

"We've got a witness, a Mr. Proudie, who keeps the antique shop on the corner. He'll testify as to identity."

"What was the idea in buying the natty scarf set?" asked Crook curiously.

"I thought if she recognized me at once she'd shut the door in my face. I hoped I'd look different. . . ."

"She'd think you'd come to mend the TV, and once inside you were going to turn the house upside down."

"The front door wasn't shut, there was no need to break in. I called out but there was no answer. I started to go through the rooms. She wasn't living there alone, you know, not all the time anyway. There were men's clothes in one of the bedrooms upstairs. . . . And then I broke open the other one, and there she was."

"Didn't think to give the alarm?"

"There was no time. I heard the steps and I thought it was this fellow coming back."

"That's an additional charge, you know," Crook warned him. "You don't believe in doing things by halves, do you? Murder and assaulting a policeman. Quite a dish."

"According to our reckoning there was fifteen minutes between the time we got the warning that someone was breaking in and our arrival," said Frost slowly. "Plenty of time to telephone."

Frank didn't argue that toss. He had no notion how long he had stood staring at that poor contorted face, shaken almost out of his wits for the first minute, fearing it might be Jan, and then letting time go over his head like water or cloud before the normal rhythm of life was restored. And by then it was too late. The police had arrived.

"Don't you have to prove a motive?" he inquired at last. "I'd never seen that girl before that day."

"That'll be enough for now," Crook assured him. "And they don't have to prove a motive anyway, though naturally it's helpful if they can. Your move, Inspector."

It turned out as Crook anticipated. He couldn't go soon enough to please the authorities, but Frank would be detained, pending inquiries. Crook had a word in virtual privacy before he took his departure.

"It could be worse," he assured his client. "I wouldn't give much for your chances of living if you were at liberty. These chaps mean for you to carry the can, and who knows if there mightn't be another Clumber roaming around the dark streets, this time a bit more successful."

"But they can't be mugs enough to suppose the police will drop a murder case because I'm in the mortuary," Frank protested.

"The police can do a lot," said Crook, "but they can't bring a dead man to trial. It could even be made to look like suicide. Chaps are very good at adding two and two, though a good many of them have never got any further."

"There's no reason why I should commit suicide," Frank protested. "I know all that stuff about the death-wish, but you can take it from me, I'm the exception that proves the rule. I *like* being alive."

Then, as Crook was going, he said it. "What are Jan's chances, Mr. Crook?"

"About the same as they were before," Crook told him. "They'll realize now I'm somewhere on the field, but they'll also know that to take any drastic step will invite the limelight for them."

All the same he knew, and so did Frank, that there were some risks even desperate men daren't take, and to release a girl who could identify her captors was one of them.

Eleven

"That chap, Darwin," observed Crook to Bill Parsons on his return to Bloomsbury Street, "I have a lot of sympathy with him hunting for his missing link. It's what I'm doing myself right now. Frank assumes that this girl Plantagenet was killed because she knew too much about the Janice Grey affair, but there's no proof at all. It's true her car was used, but if she did know it was going to be borrowed that don't mean she knew why. From what Frank tells me she sounds a Miss Blabbermouth. And then there's the missing hour. Why did X wait practically an hour before singing her to sleep with a bearlike hug?"

"If she's as dumb as you make her sound, it may have taken him an hour to decide he couldn't afford to let her go into her canary act." He did a little meditative trill. "What did she tell Frank James that could be dangerous?"

"She gave herself away by admittin' she knew Janice Grey was calling herself an actress, and Frank had the sense to see the hole in that bucket. Now say she let on to X what she'd said . . . Still, it don't seem enough. Even a gang like this one don't murder for the fun of the thing, and he couldn't know he was going to be able to pass the buck so neatly."

"It doesn't have to be anything to do with our case," Bill agreed. "This chap was presumably paying the rent. Say someone came in by the back and he found out—come to that, he may think Frank's yarn just half a yard of boloney. And didn't you say the chap hung about for the better part of an hour in a disguise that wouldn't have deceived a tom kitten?"

"Funny how all these fellows fancy themselves as mummers," Crook conceded. "You could have something there, Bill. And then he saw our young man mounting the steps, which 'ud dot a lot of i's and cross a lot of t's, and he thought, Here's my chance, and he nipped in and called the police. It's a very nice theory and could be the truth, only like that old boy on the box once remarked, justice must not only be done but also be seen to be done, meaning truth ain't enough until you can prove it's the truth."

"Didn't you say X was in the box when Frank climbed the stair? He wasn't ringing the police then."

"Warning the gang the girl might have spilled the plot. Or giving instructions about Janice Grey. Or even telling 'em to keep their eyes peeled for young Frank. Your guess is as good as mine. There's one thing, though. It might be worth while tryin' to find out if a toll call was put through from that box this afternoon. If it wasn't and he was contacting the gang, then it could mean the girl's still in the Greater London area." He scowled. "Too many conditional tenses about this case, Bill."

An hour later they knew that no long-distance call had been made from that particular number during that afternoon.

"The car was seen in the Mill Hill area," Crook brooded. "The car wasn't reported missing till after its number had been taken. We don't know how long it was before the cop made his report—about the crossing incident, I mean. Once it was known that the car was hot, they wouldn't have used it a minute longer than they had to. After all, a Clumber isn't so easily overlooked. You know, Bill, this is getting us nowhere. We'd better go into our usual routine and see what gives."

Bill saw that Crook was really apprehensive for the girl's safety. What was more he was showing it, which was proof of how apprehensive he was. North London, as both knew, has as many empty and derelict houses as any other part of the borough. Many were reduced to shells by enemy bombing and were scheduled for demolition, but until the authorities chose to take responsibility for them, there they'd stand. Tramps slept there and they were an open invitation to sex maniacs and a danger to young children. They had basements and back gardens, and some might be near a canal.

"That Miss Grey can have been dead for days, Bill," acknowledged Crook painfully. "Come to think of it, there's no blooming reason I can fathom why she should still be alive."

As a matter of routine, the police had given the house in Spring Terrace the usual check. Whatever the reason for the crime, it hadn't been theft. They found the Plantagenet girl's bag with about fifteen pounds in notes, a nice diamond ring she'd been wearing was still on her finger—no wedding ring, they noted—and there were other pieces of jewelry, mostly diamonds, in a case in her room. Diamonds are a readier form of exchange, if you know your way around, than stocks or shares, and ownership doesn't have to be stated. They had also found a torn cigar band, which bore out Frank's statement about the man smoking a cigar when he left the house. But several thousand people smoke similar cigars, and in any case Crook hadn't needed any proof of Frank's statement. He was more inclined to believe that the murder might have been the result of a private man-girl affair. The time factor alone seemed to point in that direction. A man accustomed to taking big decisions, as the gang had certainly done, would hardly spend the better part of an hour discussing details with a nitwit like Dina Plantagenet. The trouble, of course, was that the only person who could have supplied answers to his problem wasn't talking. On the other hand, if he'd had reason to suppose she was the weak link in the chain, this chap wouldn't allow any romantic consideration to stop him destroying the link.

He'd put inquiries out as to the ownership or tenancy of No. 8 but these didn't get him far. He learned that the four houses on this side of the terrace had suffered badly in the war and had subsequently been bought up by an enterprising speculator, who had transformed them from the workmen's cottages they had been originally and sold them, no doubt at a pretty handsome profit, to private buyers. No. 8 had been bought by a man who gave his name as Smith. The deal had been transacted through a third party and Smith himself had not put in an appearance. This third party was a man called Forster, who had had a small house agency in Vickers Street, but this had closed the previous year when the offices were scheduled for demolition as part of a road-widening process. Forster had vanished, taking all his records with him. Someone remembered vaguely hearing him speak of emigrating—so no soap there.

At the tax office he learned that the taxes had been paid in cash, and no one recollected precisely who had paid them. Neighbors thought the Plantagenet girl had been living there for about eighteen months. It was understood that the owner had let the place furnished. Presumably the lady had paid her rent direct—always assuming that any rent had been demanded.

"We can go on like this and meet ourselves going to bed," objected Crook.

"Try the char," suggested Bill. "These sluts never clean their own places."

But the late Miss Plantagenet hadn't employed a regular char. A firm of house cleaners had called once a week for a time, but the arrangement had been canceled some months previously.

"They're only pocket-handkerchiefs of houses," said the manager of Housemen, Limited. "A girl with no job could easily do the work herself."

Crook got a man to go down and see what he could find out. "Send Fielding," Bill advised. "He has a way with him could wangle a penny out of a closed money box."

The trouble was that hardly anyone seemed really interested in the crime. Murder's not what it was; there are so many other matters to engage the public attention, bomb threats and wars all over the world, violence on the increase everywhere, and even the press aren't allowed to fill their pages with the kind of salacious detail that titillates the imagination. To Spring Terrace she was a girl who hadn't known enough to come in out of the rain, and that was that. She had never made the grade theatrically, and anyone who's had a six-line part in a play is entitled to describe herself as an actress. So she could hardly hope at this stage to be front-page news. Nobody, except Crook and possibly the police, tied her up with the far more interesting case of Janice Grey. There were, in fact, only two interesting things about her: she'd owned a Clumber—it was registered in her name—and she'd got herself murdered. Trying to have her cake and eat it too was the general verdict.

Turning into Spring Terrace from the crowded and often shabby streets that surrounded it was like walking into an oasis. These four houses might have been reconstructed with a minimum regard to regulations, but they looked as pretty as a picture. All the doors were painted a different color and decorated with fancy knockers; the basements were rechristened garden floor, and pots of shrubs and stands of plants darkened the lower windows. They made an odd contrast to the four houses on the other side of the road, that were still being used as working-class dwellings. When Crook's man Fielding turned into this little by-street he got the impression that the place was inhabited by sleeping princesses whose hundred years wasn't yet up. If there were any kids in the houses with uneven numbers, they were still in school. Mum was probably out working or having a snooze in the back parlor. No ancient head nodded at him from a window or watched secretly from behind a curtain. He found it quite eerie, and was relieved when a plane rushed past in the bright sky, making a noise like a million angry bees. No traffic, no eyes anywhere—perhaps they slept all day and only came to life at night, like owls—not even a radio blaring. He even started looking for a church in case he'd got into a cemetery by accident.

Suddenly the door of No. 3 opened. He didn't see it because he was concentrating on the other side of the road.

" 'Aving a look at the murder house, duck?" inquired a sly, cracked voice.

He swung around. A bedraggled, yet lively figure grinned at him from about shoulder-level.

"It doesn't look much different from the rest," he offered.

"Don't suppose it was much different, not till she got herself killed. Not very nice for us, was it, but they never think of that." She spoke as if getting yourself killed was an act of carelessness, like breaking a saucer.

"Did you know her?" murmured Fielding, pulling out his cigarettes and offering her one.

"You shouldn't tempt me," the crone reproved him, but out came her skinny claw. "Sticks of death they call 'em, don't they? Thanks, dear," as he struck a match and bent to give her a light. "What was that you were saying? You'll excuse me asking, but you're new here, aren't you, dear?"

"I don't know London very well," Fielding excused himself mendaciously.

"Thought not. I don't know how it is in the country"—she made the country sound like the mountains of the moon—"but round 'ere we don't ask questions. Live and let live, see? I knew 'er by sight, of course," she added, relenting at the appeal in his humble, hopeful face. " 'Er trouble was she didn't know when she was well off. But there, that's girls all over these days. Not," she added, with an alarming gin-sodden wink, "that we was so different. After all, you're only young once."

"Only some of us," suggested Fielding, realizing some comment was called for, "stay young longer than others."

She gave him a poke with a bony elbow that nearly drove the breath out of his body.

"Friend of yours?" she inquired.

"I never met her. Of course, I might have seen her on the stage. . . ."

"They should put your picture in the Sunday papers if ever you did. Well, why should she work for a living when someone was waiting to hand it to her on a plate. Only wish I 'ad 'er chances."

She looked down at her skinny little cockatoo body and chuckled.

"What was *he* like?" Fielding murmured idly.

At once he realized he'd made a mistake. "Now that, dear,

is something I wouldn't tell you if I knew. People 'ave a right to their privacy. If she chose to 'ave a friend, that was 'er concern. And if she chose to 'ave another friend, well, if you ask me, that was 'er bad judgment. Off with the old love before you're on with the new, that's always been my motto. Still, there it is. They do say variety is the spice of life."

"Box and Cox?" suggested Fielding amiably.

"I never 'eard either of their names," said the old witch swiftly. "And if you knew, what were you askin' me for?" She seemed suddenly to be clothed in umbrage. "And if you're a copper," she wound up, allowing the tides of wrath to sweep her out to sea, "it 'ud 'ave been more gentlemanly to say so right off." With a dramatic gesture she cast away the almost-smoked cigarette and set a misshapen shoe on the glowing end. "Anyway," she added weakly, "I thought they'd got the chap that done it."

"Even the police can be wrong."

"You can say that again."

He wondered what form her particular trouble had taken. Shoplifting? Creating a disturbance after closing hours? Not above a bit of blackmail, he reflected.

"Still, 'e asked for it," she went on. "'Anging round 'er. 'E wasn't the one that paid the rent."

The door of No. 3 opened again; a younger woman, but still no spring chicken, appeared on the step.

"Gran!" screeched a voice. "Are you at it again? You don't 'ave to mind 'er, sir. She don't mean no 'arm." The woman came down the steps and grabbed the old woman by the arm. "Sorry if she's been bothering you. She gets ideas."

"'E didn't give me nothing," insisted the old woman furiously. "Nothing but a bleeding fag, and not even one of the tipped sort."

The younger woman dragged her away. So that was it, reflected Fielding. Making a nuisance of herself by begging. Well, she hadn't begged anything off him. In a way, he felt he owed her something.

The door of No. 3 clashed noisily, a boy rode a bicycle into the Terrace and hung a packet of cat's meat on a knocker and pedaled cheerfully off again. Then a window cleaner came with his ladder and mounted the steps of No. 2. But no one answered his bell and he came back to the street, looking disgruntled.

Window cleaner, thought Fielding. He might know something.

"No one at home?" he offered, once again producing his cigarettes.

"Or otherwise occupied. 'Ere, there's no sense your waiting outside No. 8. That's where that girl was clobbered."

"I know," Fielding said. "I was trying to find out something about her. No, I'm not a policeman. Acting for the defense. You know they've taken a chap?"

"Beats me why there has to be all this fuss when a tramp gets herself done in," retorted the window cleaner. "You take it from me, mate, most of the people that get themselves murdered—not counting kids, of course, and hanging's too good for that kind—but the others, they ask for it. Some of these wives—nag and worry, worry and nag, never any end to it till one day some poor devil picks up the poker, and then . . ."

"I'm single myself," offered Fielding, who could vary his domestic conditions according to his audience.

"You're lucky, mate. You're dead lucky. If I was still single you wouldn't catch me emptying trash cans and taking messages—no justice anywhere, if you ask me. All this one had to do was lie on her back and the air rained diamonds. Well, didn't you know? I can believe a lot but not that a girl uses a shaving brush and hairbrushes with ebony backs. Out on the dressing table as bold as brass. Oh, my father must have left those when he was up one night last week, she tells me. I daresay he'll be sending for them."

"I wonder she bothered to explain."

"Makes me sick. Know what I get for this job? Seven and bloody six an hour, that's what it works out at. By the time I've paid my insurance and pension, what's left? And she don't work above an hour or two in the twenty-four and she can drive a stinking great car—know what those Clumbers cost?"

Fielding shook his head. "I drive a Miniminor myself."

"I drive a motorbike, when the boy 'asn't 'helped 'imself. There's justice for you." He rested the foot of the ladder on the pavement. "Seven and bloody six," he repeated. "All these foreigners work for that."

"Mind your language," exclaimed Fielding. "That's how riots start."

"See what I mean? No freedom of speech now. Here I am in my own country and I can't speak my mind without some jumped-up cop telling me to mind my speech."

"I've told you, I'm not a policeman. I'm just trying to find out something about the dead girl. Who was she? Where did she come from? Who staked her to the house? Who paid for the car? Come to that, who's got it now?"

"Why ask me? Chap who paid for it, I suppose. Daresay the car 'ull be back before long. Like a blooming bird cage," he went on, sourly. "Get yourself a canary. When the cat gets the canary, get yourself a parakeet. Yes, and I'll be cleaning the windows and emptying the garbage, I daresay, and running the errands."

"If you dislike it so much, why do it?" asked Fielding reasonably.

"My wife's got to live. And that's where the money is—what you might call the side lines. See?"

"I see," agreed Fielding, rather grimly. "Well, the laborer's worthy of his hire, isn't he?"

The man's ice-blue eyes, faded, small, mean, acquisitive, glared into his.

"And what if the girl did put 'er 'and in 'er pocket now and again—well, it wasn't 'er money, was it?"

"You're going to miss her, aren't you?" said Fielding, with cheerful loathing.

"They're all cut to the same pattern. You'd think they'd have more sense. Taking up with foreigners, too. And asking, 'Oh, Flowers, what's your wife like? Could she wear this, do you think?' Some rag she was tired of. 'My wife doesn't care for second-hand clothes,' I told her. 'Why don't you try that place on the corner?' "

"Did she?"

" 'Ow should I know? Must ha' thought me a fool, though. Listen, mate. There was this ring on 'er dressing table, big red stone, very la-dee-da. 'You want to be careful how you leave your things lying about,' I told her. 'It 'ud never do to go losing that, would it?' Probably say I'd taken it and all."

"For your wife?" breathed Fielding.

The man grinned for the first time, showing a horrible array of fangs. "Well, it wasn't exactly what you'd call a lady's ring. That's why I said foreigners, see. 'Oh, I picked that up in the Portobello Road,' she said. Cool as a cucumber. 'Thought I could have it altered to fit me.' And then a long spiel about how when she was an ingénue—whatever that may be—she'd played some queen's part and wore a ring like this. 'Of course, it's only a garnet,' she said. 'Not valuable, but it just caught my fancy.' Well, it didn't catch 'er fancy for long. No sign of it next time I come. 'Done anything about the ring?' I asked her. 'Oh, I gave it away,' she said. I wouldn't mind knowing who's wearing it now."

In No. 2 a window curtain moved; a head shook and the curtain fell back into place.

"I must be going," said Fielding abruptly. What he'd learned might be quite valuable. The trouble was there wasn't a jury in the land who'd believe a word Flowers said, not even under oath.

"Really," said Crook characteristically, "the primrose path is so beset with thorns you wonder they don't all opt for the lilies of virtue. Blackmail, of course. You're probably right he wouldn't cut any ice in the box, and the prosecution would point out that if we had to rely on that sort of witness . . . Interesting about the ring, though. When I was talking to the little lady on the train she happened to mention that the chap who tried to push her out was wearing a ring and it cut her lip. Could be coincidence, of course, but again, it might not. This chap with the ring was in the gang; he might have got the idea he'd like to split with X in more ways than one."

"And X found out?"

"Why not? This chap—what's his improbable name?—

Flowers—found out. I wonder what he took her to town for. Well, the story's a gift for the moralists who're lucky if they can run to a second-hand jalopy, while she runs a Clumber. . . . You know, if she hadn't had the car . . ." He struck his hands together and a picture fell off the wall. "That's it," he exclaimed. "How come I never thought of that before? Who would you say had the car now?"

"Assuming she didn't leave a will, it 'ud go to the next of kin."

"Exactly. The next of kin. Think. Someone must have identified her. There must be some relative or friend. It's a funny thing in this case, every character seems to be like that perishing cat that walked alone. Pat Wylie had no family, the missing girl's got no family, young Frank's a one-only—both parents killed by a bomb in the war, and now this Dina Plantagenet. What did she get herself born, by the way?"

"Doris Prout," said Bill laconically.

"It's going to be too bad if she was a lonely orphan, too. Bill, find out who went to the mortuary. That might be a lead and heaven knows we need one. The amount of straw we've got to make bricks in this case would have made the faces of the Israelites turn red."

Twelve

The body had been identified by a sister, a Mrs. Morland, living in the Midlands. Crook got out the Superb and drove up to see her. Mr. Morland was a tall, thin, courteous man, so vague in his manner Crook would hardly have been surprised to find him walking on the ceiling instead of the carpet. Mrs. Morland was instantly on the defensive. She didn't want to talk about her sister, but if she must, then she certainly didn't want to talk about her to Mr. Crook.

"Madam," said Crook, with elaborate courtesy, "a young man's awaiting trial for the murder of your sister."

"You can hardly ask me to sympathize with him," she retorted.

"My job is to show he didn't do it, and, if I can't do that, at least get him the benefit of the doubt."

"I know nothing of my sister's affairs," Mrs. Morland declared. "We hadn't met for about two years—our ways lay widely apart—and then, after so long, to see her as she was—that monster . . ." She choked.

"Very distressing. I'm out to get him, Mrs. Morland. Tell me, do you have any idea of the name of the man who owned 8 Spring Terrace, where your sister was killed?"

"I've told you, I know nothing of Doris's affairs. Except that he treated her very shabbily, very dishonestly. In short, he deceived her."

"Under promise of marriage?" Surely that old pussy wasn't still being hauled out of the sack?

"She certainly believed he intended to marry her. Mind you, I always thought him too old, but I understood he could provide for her, and sometimes an older man has a steadying influence. My sister was only twenty-seven when she died," she added, on a sob.

"And, of course, more to offer," contributed Mr. Morland in a soft, melancholy voice.

"Gerald, that's no way to speak of poor Doris. She was very disappointed not to get better parts offered her—I understand there's a great deal of jealousy on the stage . . ." She looked expectantly at her visitor.

"A great deal of jealousy everywhere," agreed Crook briskly, who hadn't been inside a theater for twenty years.

"And then theatrical people seem to live such a costly life. I mean, you have to keep up appearances and that takes money. Good clothes and taxis everywhere. And Doris liked everything to be of the best."

"Who doesn't?" asked Crook.

"I don't," said Mrs. Morland simply. "I wouldn't even be comfortable in a Clumber. Doris was terribly proud of it. She sent us a photograph of it with her at the wheel."

"Don't forget the generous donor," put in Gerald Morland. "Standing by like an English gentleman, indicating Exhibit A."

(Crook remembered one of his rum old girls confiding to him, in a moment of crisis. "And in that instant, Mr. Crook, I felt I could levitate, simply levitate, I was so excited." He felt like levitating now.)

"You never actually met him?"

"Oh no. She could hardly bring him here, my husband wouldn't have stood for that, not when we knew he couldn't marry her, I mean. It's not fair to put temptation in people's way, you never know the other person's breaking point. I've always imagined she'd reached the point of no return. I did say, 'He may be able to support you, but are you sure he'll understand you?' But you couldn't move her."

Crook began to feel his toes lifting from the well-worn carpet.

"You'd still have that photo handy?" he whispered.

"Oh, I haven't seen it for a long time. I really didn't like to think about my sister. When we were young she was always the one to attract attention, she did everything a little better than I did, recited with more feeling, got the leads in amateur theatricals, while I was always the maid, saying, 'This way, please.' And now and again a comic aunt, but that had to be played down, because there were always so many aunts in the audience, and aunts are so frequently comic."

"Do you think," said Crook, speaking as though, if he raised his voice, some priceless bird or butterfly would elude him, "you could lay your hands on it?"

"It'll be somewhere, I suppose, but honestly, Mr. Crook, is all this necessary? I mean, poor Doris is dead. . . ."

"And Mr. Crook is here to try and prevent a second death, or a life sentence, which to my mind would be worse. Maud, my dear, go and look for that photograph."

"There won't be any publicity, will there, Mr. Crook? You see, I have to think of the children."

"In less than twenty years' time our son will be the age of this young man they've taken for the murder," said Mr. Morland.

Crook was staggered to realize that he really was in command of the facts. Only showed you shouldn't judge a man by his appearances.

"Brian would never get mixed up in anything like this. How can you say such a thing, Gerald?"

"He's not a fairy child, he could get caught like anyone else."

"Brian comes from a good home."

"Didn't your sister come from a good home?"

"Mrs. Morland," said Crook desperately, "this is a case where time may not be only money but life itself. There's a girl mixed up in this, too. So if you can find that picture . . ."

After Mrs. Morland had gone, rather reluctantly, to turn out her escritoire, Gerald Morland said in his colorless voice,

"Doris was never any good. I don't sympathize with the modern trend of excusing evil on the ground of psychological maladjustment. It's much simpler than that. We accept the fact, however much we may regret it, that some infants are born minus a limb or some physical sense. Why can't we accept the equally obvious fact that some of them are born devoid of moral sense, and must be regarded as expendable? We regard murderers as expendable, and in wartime we regard soldiers as expendable, so why all this respect for someone like my sister-in-law. Even if your client was guilty, Mr. Crook, I should be shocked to think he would have to pay a final price for—blotting her out. Surely you agree with me?"

Crook had been listening with an air of great intentness. Another balding old eagle, he thought, talking through his hat. Who did he imagine he, Crook, was? The angel on the gate? Justice holding the scales? All that affected Crook were the facts that a man he was representing had been accused of murder and a girl, about whom precious little seemed to be known, had disappeared and, for all any of them knew, might already have been regarded as expendable by her captors.

But he put on a very sensible expression and said that without the facts—and he hadn't got them—he couldn't express an opinion. The mixture as before, of course, but in his game you couldn't afford to miss a trick.

Mrs. Morland came back with the photograph. It was a fair-sized snapshot, showing the excited, downbent face of a girl in a wide hat, who was sitting at the wheel of a large white car. By the hood stood a big brute of a chap, with showman written all over him. Crook reminded himself that women often liked these overpowering types; and he wasn't exactly bad-looking. Big hands, he thought, butcher's hands, hands that 'ud squeeze a girl's windpipe as easily as it 'ud wring a chicken's neck.

"Did she ever mention his name?" he asked, still staring at the picture. He knew a lot of London's underworld, though he couldn't place this chap. Still, Bill knew even more and had contacts even Crook couldn't have established.

"Doris called him Binkie."

"Oh no," Crook roared. "She can't have had all her marbles. I mean—Binkie!"

"It's probably the name his mother called him," suggested Morland, in his sober, unedifying way.

"So he has an Oedipus complex? Well, that ain't going to stop him swinging, not if I have any say in the matter. Thanks a lot, Professor. I'll be back for lesson two soon as I have the time to spare. Don't worry about the photograph, Mrs. Morland. You shall have it back."

Binkie! he thought, pouring himself into his car and belting back to London.

He found Bill at his post, full of exciting news about an attempted murder made to look like suicide (unsuccessful), a shrewd bit of wire-pulling to defraud the income tax, a juicy blackmail case, and someone who knew strangers crept into her house after dark. The last one tempted him, but he only shook his head.

"They'll all have to wait. Bill, take a look at this." He handed over the photograph Mrs. Morland had given him. "Ever seen that chap before?"

"I've been out of the line for so long," murmured Bill apologetically. "On the side of the angels, Crook's angels, that is . . ."

"Think you could find out?"

"I could try. Tricky, though. Even if he is recognized, you can't expect a chap to squeal. Here, wait a minute." He pulled open a drawer and produced a magnifying glass. Crook watched him in silence, knowing he wouldn't have let himself be hustled if the house was on fire. "Look for yourself," Bill offered, handing print and glass across.

"I've practically licked the print off the paper," Crook explained, "but I never set eyes on him before."

"I didn't suppose you had. But it wouldn't surprise me if he'd had a face-lift fairly recently. When was that taken?"

"About eighteen months ago, I suppose. That's when the girl moved into Spring Terrace. Mrs. M. said they hadn't met for about two years." He bent over the photograph. "You mean those tiny marks on the face—how can you be sure?"

"It was quite a thing in the old days—if you meant to stay alive, that is. Wonderful what a difference skin-grafting makes to your appearance. Look, I'll take this around and see what I can pick up. He's not likely to have taken a girl like that to locals. Might play it obliquely. Ask if anyone recognizes her. Not that anyone could, just a hat and a cheek-line . . ."

Crook left him to it. He shelved the Grey-James affair for the time being and was soon up to his big ears in something else.

It was more than twenty years since Bill had been one of the decorations of the law-breaking community, but in his time he had had few equals. The younger generation only knew him by name, when the old 'uns started one of their dreary reminiscing sessions—there used to be a chap called Bill Parsons—but some of his contemporaries were still on the lay and making quite a good thing out of it.

"How's the heel, Bill?" they'd ask with a wink. It had been a bullet in the heel causing a slight permanent limp that was responsible for Bill's retirement from a profession where you can't afford even so minor a disability.

Now he drifted first into The White Knight and ordered a Scotch and water. There were pubs where you learned what you wanted on beer, and others on whiskey. This was a whiskey pub. The man behind the bar was a stranger to him, and Bill saw no one he knew. Fashions change in pubs as in everything else. He had a second Scotch and bought a drink for the landlord before he produced his photograph.

"Ever seen the girl?" he asked.

The landlord stiffened. "What's your interest?"

"Her husband's out again and looking for her," said Bill, promptly. "She ought to be warned."

The landlord looked at the picture more closely. "That the husband?"

"Not precisely."

"I'd say it was the husband who'd better watch his step. No, never saw either of them."

"Well, if she should turn up, pass the word along," said

Bill. He nodded and went out. Funny thing, the landlord told his wife later, there was something about her—only you couldn't see her properly—but I did get the idea I'd seen her somewhere. Trouble is all these dames look alike. All I hope is she don't come here. We don't want trouble."

Bill tried a couple more whiskey pubs without drawing blood anywhere. Then he turned his attention to some with a more specialized clientele, where mysterious appointments are made and codes exchanged, and where strangers aren't welcome. They all knew him in these parts as being allied to Arthur Crook, and accepted him since there was no knowing when they mightn't need his services. No one here looked particularly prosperous, but a layman would have had a shock to realize how much the clientele would be worth in death taxes, if a bomb suddenly flattened the place. It didn't seem to be Bill's night. They couldn't—or wouldn't—help him at The Fried Eel or The Chicken and Pox, while at The New Pin someone suggested nastily that he might try the police.

"Be your age," advised Bill. "This chap's a con."

His luck turned a bit at The Pelican and Pie, where he saw a man he'd known in the old days. He remembered him too well to make the first advance. You could never be certain the chap hadn't turned respectable. Sometimes, mostly when they were past it, they even turned informer. Still, though conversions were many and various, few of them stuck and fewer still made a profit out of it. Lingard, however, recognized an old colleague.

"'Oo-re you goin' to meet, Bill? 'Ave you bought the street, Bill?" he murmured, passing up his tankard for another pint.

"Nice to be back," said Bill, and there was a wistful gleam in his eye. As they moved away together he added casually, "Nice job you pulled at Alcott's the other night. Took me back a long way."

"Piece of cake," said Lingard. "If you got the patience. That's what the youngsters lack. Goramighty, you'd think they were expecting the bomb before morning the way they go at a job. Remember the Salome Club, Bill? How long did we case that before we started thinking about a date?"

"Lovely grub," Bill agreed. "Mike, ever seen either of these?" He pulled out the photograph.

"I don't know the dame, but the chap—here, why d'you want to know?"

"Crook wants him—suspected murder."

"He should run a mile," said Mike reverently. "And then when he's got his breath back, another two. If Crook's made up his mind the chap may as well say his prayers. He'll just sit down and arrange the evidence like a game of drafts."

Bill looked down his long nose. "British justice the best in the world," he intoned. "Crook just wants to keep it that way."

It was an odd thing about Crook; even chaps who'd never met him had the idea it was nicer to be on the same side rather than fight across a trench. And if Bill dropped the weakest hint that there was a chap at The Pelican and Pie who might be able to come across, Crook would be like the man in the poem who never ceased from mortal strife. You'd never dare open your eyes of a morning without wondering if you'd find him sitting beside your bed.

"I can't put a name to him," said Lingard shortly. "But you could try The Looking Glass in Purchase Lane."

A nod's as good as a wink to a blind horse. Bill knew The Looking Glass had the reputation of being the headquarters of some of the most skillful jewel thieves about town. It all began to add up.

At The Looking Glass he played safe, asking about the girl. But, as though the word had gone around, no one was talking. There was a tall man along the bar who craned his neck to see the picture. Bill showed it to him.

"What's your interest?" the man demanded.

"Girl's my sister," said Bill promptly, and the barman laughed, rather the way a skeleton might.

"If you do find her you might give me an introduction," said the tall man.

There was no sign of anyone like the fellow in the photograph, but quite soon the other chap oiled off through a side door.

"Telephone?" pantomimed Bill.

"In use," said the barman shortly. "Box on the corner of Elderberry Street."

Bill, who had shifted to a place where he could see the world outside, nodded his thanks. A minute later he shot out of the pub like a rabbit with a ferret on its trail. A taxi was nosing its way up the street, and he hailed it. As it started to perform a U-turn the tall man came back from telephoning. He leaned over and said something to the barman and then came for the door. As he pulled it open Bill shot into the taxi, yelling "Waterloo" at the top of his voice. The tall man glanced around but there were no other taxicabs in sight, so he dropped down into the nearest subway. With traffic the way it was this time of day, the underground was quicker than any cab. Nosy Parker was going to get a nice surprise when he reached the station.

Once he'd turned the corner, Bill leaned forward and told the driver, "Changed my mind. 123 Bloomsbury Street."

If the driver recognized the address—and most of the night cabbies did—he gave no sign. When the cab was halted by lights Bill leaned out of the window and bought a late edition of the *Record*. The headlines read:

WESTMINSTER MURDER—NEW TRAIL

and:

MY SISTER'S SECRET LIFE

THE GIRL WHO DREAMED OF FAME

The lights were burning in Crook's office as Bill came easily up the long stairs.

"I didn't get the name," he acknowledged, "but he's known at The Looking Glass. Lying low tonight, but there was another chap who took a lot of interest in my movements. Tall fellow and—get this, Crook—wore a very fancy red ring. If I don't miss my guess he's hanging around Waterloo Station this instant, and I wouldn't be surprised to know he had a knife handy. It's to be hoped he doesn't get so annoyed he starts carving up some other chap."

He began to whistle, "O where is my wandering boy tonight?"

"Wandering boy, my foot!" ejaculated Crook. "What's worrying me is our wandering girl, and is she still above ground?"

Thirteen

In a room in Hadlington, one of London's new overspill towns, about forty miles north of Paddington, a man and a woman were talking. He was about five-and-thirty, and Emma Hiscock might have recognized him; the woman was small and neat and trim as a bird, with a round dark head as smooth as butter.

"I don't like it, Terry," she was saying in a restless, miserable voice. "I don't like it one little bit. You promised me you wouldn't get mixed up in any more of these deals."

"Don't nag, angel. I've told you this will be the last."

"They're all the last with you. And, if you're not careful, you may find you're telling the truth by accident."

"Meaning?"

"They'll catch up with you before you've time to disentangle yourself. Why don't we up stakes and go to Australia, say?"

"Why Australia?"

She moved her hands vaguely. "It's a big place. We could get lost there."

"This isn't precisely the moment to discuss emigration," he pointed out, dryly. "We're still up to our neck in this Jan Grey business."

"Neck being the operative word. How long does Harris mean this thing to drag on?"

"No one but Harris can tell you that, and, if you know your onions, you'll wait for him to speak first. He'll tell us when he's good and ready. Mind you, I don't know any more than you do what's brewing, but remember patience is one of the deadly virtues. If Pat had remembered that, he might be with us still."

"And meanwhile we hold the baby. Isn't that like him?" She moved restlessly to the window, though there was nothing to be seen except the empty road that was seldom used now except at week ends, since the authorities built the by-pass that was to serve Hadlington New Town. "I still don't understand why you brought the girl here. I thought it was all settled that she was to go to Dina."

"That was before the Clumber got so much limelight. Anyway, I never trusted that tart, can't see what Harris saw in her. Didn't he realize that the minute she shut the front door behind him she was opening the back door to the next boy friend?"

"Well, he knows it now," said the girl in a hard voice. "Though I've been wondering if he didn't mean it to be this way—to put Dina down, I mean, as if she were a dog. Oh, what's the good of looking so shocked? We both know this boy they've taken for the murder had nothing to do with it."

"I don't know anything of the kind," retorted her husband harshly, "and if you've got any sense, you won't either."

"I suppose Dina's clock went wrong or something," Susan reflected. "You'd think Harris would go for the man. Or could he really believe this Frank James is the one?"

"Sometimes, darling, you're so intelligent I wonder what's happened to the canary whose brain you've got. It's obvious where this lad's interest lies." He frowned. "Altogether too many people interested in Janice Grey. Who on earth dragged Crook into this? He must be the champion gate crasher of all time."

"And if his friend, the devil, puts him on the right track, Terry my sweet, hang onto your hat and run. You know Harris or Wilf would shoot us both before breakfast without wrecking their appetites." She came back into the room and stood there with her head lifted. "She's on the move again, you can hear her right through the house. Up and down, up and down. It gives me the willies."

"Good for the figure," said Terry callously. "She can't get out, not unless you've forgotten to lock the door, and you wouldn't do that, would you, darling?"

"I keep thinking how she must feel. She's not even as old as I am. She can't believe Harris is going to let her go. Only—what's the alternative?"

Her husband said nothing.

"Oh no, Terry," she whispered. "Not that. I mean she couldn't tell them anything helpful."

"Except, of course, that she could recognize Wilf and me—and you, of course. It's just a question of which of us comes first with you. Her or me. And now Crook's put the lid on it. If she couldn't remember a thing, he'd furnish her with a memory and persuade the jury it was the genuine article. Be your age, Susan. Harris can't take a risk like that."

"This is what he intended from the start?" Her voice was as pale as her ashen cheek.

Terry replied, as Pat had done a bare week ago, "No one intends violence. Sometimes it just happens."

"It's different for you," she cried. "To you and Wilf she's not a person at all, just a link in a chain. . . ."

"They're all links in chains," said Terry roughly. "When you start thinking of them in human terms, you're done. It's like generals; they can't think of armies as individuals, they're expendable bodies. All that matters is ending up on the winning side."

"Well, you try taking up her meals and giving her stuff to keep her quiet, and listening to her appealing to your sense of decency. It's no good, Terry. I can't go on. Let's get out, never mind the risk, let's get out now."

"Do you seriously suppose Harris would let us get as far as London, even? We're his allies, yes, but when allies let you down, they're worse than enemies. The fact is, the chips haven't fallen quite as Harris expected; he's got to try and pick them up without being picked up himself. If you want to blame anyone, blame Pat for starting all this by putting Routh out for the count."

"You talk about how far-sighted Harris is, but it wasn't very far-sighted of him to gather Pat into the bosom of the family. Oh, I daresay he was a charmer, but anyone with any sense could see he wouldn't be dependable in a crisis."

"He was all right so long as he kept his job." Doggedly Terry defended the boss. "That job of his gave him a lot of invaluable inside information, and Harris is just the chap to cash in on that. Of course, once he got sacked from that—too big for his boots and Harris warned him—well, he was no more use than anyone else; in fact, you could find half a dozen more reliable fellows over the week end."

"I suppose he thought it wasn't worth straining his guts to make a thousand pounds a year, when you realize what he must have been taking on the side."

"Well, you don't have to be sorry for him, sweetie. He asked for everything he got."

"I'm not sorry for him. It's us I'm sorry for, getting sucked into this, because the whole gang can be pulled in for murder, if it was Pat who struck the blow. And I'm specially sorry for me because one of these mornings I'm going to wake up and find I'm a widow without even a grave to take flowers to. And I'm sorry for Jan Grey, because she didn't have much fun with Pat—why on earth couldn't he have left her at St. Benyons?"

"You didn't see the letter she left for him when she ran out that first time. She knew she was doing wrong not going to the police, but he was her husband and she couldn't. But if she ever read that another man had died, she wouldn't let anything stand in her way. She meant it, too."

"How would she link up Pat with this fellow Routh?"

"There's some chances you don't take; and then when providence shoved an ace into Pat's hand—seeing her by chance that day, I mean—he'd have been a fool not to play it. Mind you, in his own way Pat had been fond of her, probably thought he could use her as a hostage and dictate terms to Harris. That shows you how crazy he was. How did she feel about him?" he added curiously. "I've often wondered."

"She hated him before the end," said Susan in quiet tones. "You can always tell. She won't even speak of him. But she must have loved him all right at the beginning. Terry, is there nothing we could do?"

"Now, don't get hysterical, Susan. That girl signed her death warrant when she married Pat. You can't imagine Harris is going to sit on his haunches and watch his life go down the drain on account of a little itsy-bitsy girl who thinks life's like the Sermon on the Mount."

"Where is he now—Harris, I mean?"

"How should I know? He's like the demon king, comes and goes in a puff of black smoke."

"Perhaps he's pushing Wilf off a station platform," Susan suggested. "He must be livid about him getting the Clumber identified. And don't think he wouldn't sell all of us down the river if it suited his book, turn Queen's Evidence . . ."

For the first time her husband showed alarm. "Good God, girl, watch that tongue of yours. If he were to hear you say that . . ."

"You mean, you'd be bringing the flowers to my grave. If it wasn't for you, you heavenly good-for-nothing slob, I'd put my hat on and go to the police now."

"Have I heard that before? It's what Jan Grey said to Pat or the equivalent."

"And she can't say fairer than that, can she?" asked a new voice from the doorway.

Both Bateses swung around, shocked at the interruption. A tall, heavily built man stood on the threshold. If Jan had been there she might have found it difficult to associate him with the heavily scarred scoundrel she had glimpsed at Victoria Station talking to Pat three years ago. Months in a convalescent home on the Continent, four separate operations and skin grafts in Switzerland, dentures to replace the irregular, tigerish teeth that had made him so conspicuous, had produced a different man. The big fleshy nose had been refined, even the shape of the eyes was changed. The young couple had sprung apart at his appearance and stood looking at him with every semblance of guilt. Harris smiled back with all the affability of a tiger after prey.

"I'm not sure what the penalty is for watchdogs that sleep at their post," he observed. "I might have been Arthur Crook." He smiled with ferocious geniality at Susan. "So you're going to the police, are you, my dear? Perhaps I could give you a lift. I've put the car in the garage, but no trouble would be too much for a nice little girl like you."

"Lay off, Harris," said Terry. "She's got an attack of that girls-together feeling."

"I'm afraid you don't trust me, Susan," Harris said in a sad voice.

"No one's luck lasts for ever," replied Susan desperately. "Mr. Harris, how much longer is Jan Grey going to be here?"

"The good general never confides in his men. Terry should have told you that. He gives the orders. Don't worry, your ordeal's almost at an end. In the meantime, even an accidental betrayal could spell disaster for us all. When you find yourself out of your depth and can't swim, the only thing to do is to tread water and—keep your mouth shut."

"I'll answer for my wife," said Terry.

"You young men! You have such assurance. Pat thought he could answer for his."

"Oh, I'm not as brave as Jan," cried Susan recklessly. "I admire her." She glanced at her watch. "It's time for her tea."

She ran across the room and Harris moved politely aside to let her go.

"Set 'em up, Terry," he said. "I fancy you and I could do with something a bit stronger than tea. In the meantime, I'd like a word with Susan. We mustn't forget this is a case of pull, pull together."

He went out and Terry could hear his heavy tread as he moved toward the kitchen where Susan was setting out a tray.

He came back alone a few minutes later. "It's a pity about your wife, Terry. I didn't expect her to turn yellow."

"Susan's not yellow. She's scared. She didn't expect marriage to be like this. Women like a settled background. . . ."

"Fifteen quid a week and payments on the washing machine," sneered Harris. "Let her try it and see how much fun that is."

"You can never tell with girls," Terry said. "Women don't make sense anyhow."

"She'd better pull herself together, unless she fancies the settled background of a churchyard. And that goes for us all. Listen, Terry. Crook's on the warpath."

"We knew that," Terry pointed out.

"How much more do you know? I don't like all this secrecy, boy. Makes a man wonder who he can trust. Things are hotting up now, all right. Parsons is getting after Wilf. He was seen at The Looking Glass, asking questions. If Wilf had been a bit smarter he wouldn't have lost sight of him and Crook would now be looking for another assistant."

"And the rest of us would be looking for the rocks to fall down and hide us," ejaculated Terry irrepressibly.

"Someone," said Harris in smooth tones, "must have tipped him off. They don't know Bill at The Looking Glass. No idea who it could be, I suppose?"

"How could I?" inquired Terry stubbornly.

"You know what those two are like when they hunt in couples. They'd be perfectly capable of putting a corpse through your front window and swearing on oath they saw you carving it up. Well, others might do that. The difference in this case is that Crook and Parsons would get away with it."

"Do they know where the girl is?"

"If they don't, you can take it from me they soon will. Now, there's nothing against a businessman renting a house in the country—if you can call this the country, and having his daughter and son-in-law to stay—that's what I said, don't gape—so long as there's no one else around. The long and the short of it is, Terry, that girl's got to go, and Susan's got to do her share. If you've any influence there, now's the time to exercise it."

Janice heard the careful feet coming up the stairs and turned swiftly toward the door. Since her arrival she had seen no one but this girl, who, since she wore a wedding ring, was clearly the wife of one of the men who had brought her here. But she knew there were other people in the house; standing by the locked door, her ear to the crack, she could distinguish different footsteps on what appeared to be uncarpeted stairs. There was a quick brisk male step, and a long, lounging one, and there might be others, she couldn't be certain. Left, right, left, right, came the feet, and halted outside the door.

"Tea?" wondered Janice, trying to remember the contents of the last tray. One of her minor torments was that her watch had stopped and no one would tell her the time. There was no radio, no church clock, and the girl herself either possessed no watch or left it behind when she came up to the attic. It wasn't even possible to make an approximate guess by surveying the sky or the movements of the world outside, because the windows of this bleak room, whose sole furnishings were a bed, a table and a chair, were securely shuttered and padlocked for good measure. You could beat the breath out of your body flailing against those and never be heard. The room was lighted by a weak electric bulb hung high in the ceiling. Sometimes, because she had so much time on her hands, Jan would imagine the watery beam was fainter yet, would be extinguished at any moment, and then she might lie in the dark, ears strained for sounds she couldn't identify, till her mind broke through the thin web of sanity. That she was at the top of the house she knew, because she could hear the intermittent rain pattering on the roof; it had been judged good enough for a servant once, this room with its faded floral paper and paint the color of weak tea. Even a housekeeper's room, she thought, since there was a windowless bathroom opening off it. The bath was chipped; there was neither chain nor plug until the girl who was her jailer brought them once a day.

Perhaps they think I'll be tempted to hang myself or drown myself or strangle myself with the chain, she reflected wonderingly. "Why on earth should they expect me to do their job for them?"

She had no notion where she was; the potion given her in the coffee had left her dazed and noncomprehending before they reached this house. Vaguely she could recall being helped or pulled up a great many stairs in a poor light. Then she had been thrust through this door and here she remained, only spacing off the hours by the trays of food that Susan brought her. Even those might be set for irregular intervals, in order to confuse her yet more.

She had listened hard but had never heard the sound of a bell or a telephone. Of course, at this height the sound might be so muffled it wouldn't penetrate the shiny varnished wooden door.

She thought about Crook quite a lot, what a fool she'd been not to keep in touch, she who had no friends. There was no one to bother about her, Miss Hiscock believed she'd gone to a new job, the cinema manager would shrug and say, Another of these unreliable girls, heard of something she liked better, I suppose. As for Crook's card, that had probably found its way to the trash heap long ago. She remembered propping it up on the mantelpiece that first evening, but it had slipped or been thrown away. And he doesn't even know my name, she thought. Of course, she could perhaps get his number through the operator.

The door opened and Susan came in, carrying a tray.

"Hungry?" she said with forced cheerfulness, setting it on the table.

"Ravenous—for a little information. Where am I?"

"You're being looked after."

"Oughtn't I to know my host's name? Is it the man with the ring?"

"I don't know anything about a man with a ring."

"He was driving the car. Which one are you married to?"

"Does it matter?"

"I should think it might—to you. Did you know the driver had already tried to kill me?"

"No." Susan turned in sudden revolt. "Why do you try and goad me? Do you suppose I'm any more of a free agent than you are? I have to take orders, too."

"Haven't I heard that somewhere before? Dachau—and Hola Camp? It doesn't hold water, you know."

"Eat your tea," Susan pleaded. "Then I can open the window and let in some fresh air. I'm sure you must be hungry."

"You're so humorous," Jan murmured. "Let's see, what have we tonight? A nice arsenic sandwich?"

"No one's trying to poison you," Susan protested. "Where on earth did you get that idea?"

"Do I sound so unreasonable? I suppose it's remembering how one of your lot murdered my husband. . . ."

"Say what you like to me," Susan warned her. "What girls tell each other is off the record, but if one of the others comes up, watch your step."

"How many others are there?"

Susan shot her a quick glance. "At the moment they're all out, but I expect you'll see them soon."

"Oh, come on," Jan encouraged her. "Let your hair down for once. Or does someone stand outside the door eavesdropping all through the day? Or perhaps there's a microphone hidden in the walls. There always is in spy stories—Pat used to love them, I wish now I'd read them more carefully, but they were never my cup of tea. I've been round and round, tapping the walls, looking for a weak place that leads to the secret stairway. What a shock your friends would have if I suddenly poked up my head from a floorboard. Tell me, why are they keeping me here? What do they think I know?"

"Where's the sense in asking me?"

"They can't think it's anything of immense importance or they'd have taken more stringent steps to wrest my secret from me. You know, burning cigarettes on the back of your neck or pins under your fingernails."

"This isn't a concentration camp," Susan burst out.

"I daresay they got quite a lot of hints from reading about them, though."

"You're in a very talkative mood today."

"Man's a conversational animal and woman even more so. And I don't have a lot of company here. Aren't you going to open the window? It's my only proof that I'm still in the same world."

The view from the window was hardly cheering, an overgrown garden with blackened stalks drooping in the untended beds, rough lawns that hadn't been cut in months, a wild tangle of orchard and beyond that—what? It was anyone's guess. It might be the end of the world. But at least a current of fresh air blew into the room, though so far she had never heard a bird's note or even a barking dog.

Susan turned rather languidly toward the window. Jan filled a teacup and clattered it noisily on its saucer. Her heart was thudding till she thought the other girl must hear it. Because she had during this past minute realized something that was out of true. Every afternoon when Susan came in, she kicked the door shut, and dumped the tray on an adjacent table. Clearly she had been told to take no unnecessary risk. Fishing the door-key out of her pocket, she would relock the door and return the key. But this afternoon, engrossed and distrait for some reason Jan couldn't fathom, she had left the key in the door. While she spoke, Jan's eyes fastened hungrily on the key. They're all out, Susan had said. Susan herself was having trouble with the bar of the shutter.

"I don't believe these have been used for twenty years," she said crossly.

"So people don't live here all the time?" Jan put down the cup and took two cautious steps toward the door. "What is it really? A kind of disused bastille?"

"Just a house," said Susan. "Damn, there goes a fingernail."

"Why, there's a bird calling." Jan moved a few steps nearer the door. "What kind?"

"How should I know? It's just a bird."

"Frank would have known. Oh, he's just someone I met in London a long, long time ago."

With the last words, that she spoke in a louder voice, she had crossed the room, seized the key, turned it—thank goodness the lock was well-oiled—and then she was outside on the drab square landing with its varnished grained doors and hideous metal handles, and the stairs stretched down and down. . . .

She turned the key in the lock and ran. Down the attic flight, her feet clattered on bare boards, across a landing—through the window another glimpse could be obtained of the dismal landscape, with the shadows gathering like ghostly sheep —past a series of closed doors. Her heart bumping and crashing, in case one might open, she reached the main staircase, with old-fashioned Brussels carpeting, bright red and green and blue, all worn threadbare now, and then the hall.

Susan had begun to batter on the locked door.

"Batter away," she whispered. "You won't break that down." And perhaps they would even think it was she who was creating all this commotion and wouldn't realize their mistake till they came to look for Susan.

Through an open door she saw a telephone, and stopped an instant. But this room was empty like all the rest. There wasn't a sound to be heard anywhere but her own panting heart.

Fourteen

Crook had just returned to his office when his telephone began to ring. When he took off the receiver he heard a girl's breathless voice.

"Mr. Crook? This is Janice Grey. You remember? We met on the train. . . ."

"Where are you speaking from?" demanded Crook, characteristically cutting the cackle.

"I don't know. They didn't tell me. . . ."

"What's your number? Go on, it'll be on the instrument."

"Oh yes. Of course. Hadlington 129. But I'm getting out, I'll go to the police, I'll . . . No." The voice stopped abruptly. Crook thought he detected a kind of wail—dismay? horror? pain?

"Hi, sugar," he shouted. "Sugar!"

The telephone went dead. Crook put back the receiver and began to work out sums.

In the small room at Hadlington the big man faced the girl. She hung onto the edge of the table and her whole body shook.

"Talk about acting!" said Harris, admiringly. "You'll have given Mr. Crook the idea that you don't like our company. Now, stop shaking like a leaf." He put an authoritative hand on her arm. "What on earth have you got to be afraid of?"

The girl didn't speak; she seemed to have exhausted all her

energy in those few words she had been allowed on the telephone.

"Know the weakness of a mouse hole?" Harris went on. "It can let the mouse escape into the room, but it can't guarantee that the door will be open."

The girl gave him a dreadful glance, compounded of such horror and helplessness as must have melted any heart but his. But he was contemplating the future and he smiled.

Crook was talking to Bill. "Hold the fort," he said. "I've just had a call. Got to go down to Hadlington."

"Watch your step," counseled Bill.

"You sound like my old granny," scoffed Crook, who'd never known any such person. "All this watching your step in case you fall over your own feet, and what happened? Some dirty great stone falls on your head and you don't see it coming because you're so busy making certain you don't stumble."

He pulled on his big brown overcoat and added, "Get Miss Hiscock on the phone and ask her if she thinks she'd recognize the chap who came calling and pretended to be the police."

Miss Hiscock said she might know him and again she might not. She couldn't recall any special moles, cicatrices, or missing finger joints. He'd been clean-shaved, but she didn't remember what he wore.

"Ask her about the voice," advised Crook, but Miss Hiscock said there wasn't anything special about that; he'd sounded like a policeman. Just as she might have said he sounded like a foreigner.

"All the same, she might know it again if she heard it. Voices give more people away than faces. Tell her to go to work on that memory of hers, and then to stand by till I give her the word."

He whirled away down the stairs, got into the old Superb with all the panache of a crusader mounting his steed, chain mail and all, and was gone.

The new town of Hadlington bore about as much relation to the original village as present-day whiskey to the 1914 variety. It shone with white paint and red brick and immense glass supermarkets, and its people lived for the most part in towering blocks of flats, each about as individual as a bee in a hive. No cinema, since they've more or less been put out of business by the telly, but a bingo hall and a *palais de danse,* and rather more espresso bars than pubs. The whole place made Crook feel like Rip Van Winkle. The old village hovered uncertainly on the outskirts, the kind of place, he thought, where the bus runs once a fortnight and the vicar's thankful if he can rake up two pewsful of worshipers on a Sunday. But it had a cozy little bar, called the Duck and Daisy, and he stopped for a drink and a little information there. The beer was quite something and no one looked at the Superb as if they suspected him of robbing the British Museum.

It was easy enough to discover the address of Hadlington 129. "Old Hadlington Manor," said the landlord. "Not much use to us. London chap, brings down a party now and again, I believe, doesn't live here, of course. The place stands empty half the year. It'll come down one of these days. Meantime it's let furnished if anyone's interested."

His tone implied that this didn't happen often.

"Bring their own supplies," he added disgustedly, "and the same goes for the food."

"Hampers from Fortnum?" suggested Crook intelligently. "What do they do about milk?"

If you wanted information, the tradesfolk were your best bet, was his experience. But it seemed they weren't much interested in milk.

Crook nodded. It was the first good thing he'd heard about them. He didn't go much for milk himself. The world's best drink, caroled his TV advertisements about three days a week, but who am I, demanded Crook, that I should have the best of anything?

"How about the young lady? I take it there is a young lady there?"

"If there wasn't," said the landlord dryly, "they'd have invented her."

From which Crook deduced that the standing of the Manor's present occupants wasn't very high locally. He had one more visit to pay before going there himself and, having got his directions, he approached the house cautiously, believing there's never any harm in taking stock of your situation before you challenge it.

Hadlington Manor wasn't a testimony to any architectural genius, being a big bare-faced brick house, with a slab of untended garden in front and what looked like a regular no man's land at the back. The nearest building was a gaunt Norman church; presumably the original owner had been one of those cheery old-world aristocrats who don't want another human creature—bar his domestic slaves—within earshot. The back door was paradoxically at the side of the building, down a lane almost as untended as the front lawn. A large double garage had been erected here, probably on the site of the original coach house. Crook cruised gently in its direction but before he got there the garage door opened and a big gray car was driven out. It came straight across his path and stopped dead.

"You should see an oculist, what with the National Health and all," yelled Crook to the driver. "What do you think this is that I've got here? A flying carpet?"

The driver paid no attention; he was a big man with a dark hat pulled over his face.

"Have it your own way," said Crook philosophically, and prepared to back out. But at that moment a third car, small and dark, turned the corner and ranged up behind him. So there he was, hemmed in between the two of them. For a moment he considered the possibilities of continuing to back; the Superb could make mincemeat of that little tin pram, but he supposed that if he did, the driver of the big gray car would come straight for him. And the Superb was a lady and you didn't subject a lady, who was also the darling of your heart, to such murderous treatment. And when the police arrived, as they would, he'd be in no position to make a statement.

This Is Your Life, reflected Mr. Crook piously. Chapter the last? he wondered. He hoped not. He liked long yarns himself, and he was prepared to see this one continue for another decade or two before someone wrote finis. So he braked again and sat peaceably where he was and waited for one of the others to make the first move.

The driver of the big car got out, and he didn't hurry himself; he came casually up to the window of the Superb and Crook could see him pretty clearly now, despite the approaching dusk. But just to make sure, he flashed on a light and the chap jumped like a dog in a circus.

My guardian angel turning up trumps as usual, decided Crook. Because if he hadn't seen this face in the flesh before, he hadn't any doubt whose it was. He'd seen its replica in a photograph handed to him by the sister of the late Doris Prout.

It was a large face and brutal, displaying about as much compassion as a man-eating tiger, with none of the tiger's agility or grace.

"What the hell do you think you're doing here?" its owner demanded.

"Parking," replied Mr. Crook. "If I'm in a zone you've only to say so. I don't expect to be here more than a couple of hours. It's an interesting fact," he went on chattily, "that more chaps get themselves murdered by outstaying their welcome than any amateur would believe."

"This is a private drive," said the man-eating tiger.

"You should put up a notice—that it is a drive, I mean. You can't expect us poor townees to know the difference."

"Terry, just come here a moment. Isn't this the chap who's been hanging around and behaving in a suspicious manner for the last couple of days?"

"I take back what I said about the oculist," apologized Crook handsomely. "If you could see me forty miles away you're a dead loss to the profession." He put his hand in his pocket and whipped out a card. "Identity papers," he offered, handing it over.

"Mr. Crook," said the big man. "Well, isn't that a surprise?"

"Is it?" murmured Crook. "I rather thought this might be the reception committee."

"Visiting in the neighborhood?" inquired Harris.

"You've got it first time. I've called to see Miss Grey."

"You've been misinformed. There's no Miss Grey here."

Crook let his eyes range over the side of the big ugly house.

"Quite a mansion," he offered. "Well, maybe you haven't noticed her. But she rang me on the phone this morning, and don't tell me you ain't Hadlington 129, because I checked before I came along."

Harris tossed Crook's card back into his lap. "If you don't believe me, come in and see for yourself."

"Very civil of you, I don't mind if I do," said Crook.

He hopped out of the Scourge and locked the door.

"Here, you can't do that," objected Harris. "My friend wants to garage his car."

"Oh come," protested Crook, "I told you I shan't be here long. Won't do her any harm to sit out for a bit. Quite a nice night," he added.

"I'll get mine out of the way," offered Harris patiently. "Then you can move down a bit, and the other car can be garaged for the night."

Crook considered the proposal; it didn't appeal to him. He could see no reason why, once the big car was out of the road, the little chap behind him shouldn't put his car into gear and send it careering after the old Rolls. It wouldn't simply smash the Rolls, the odds were it would also smash the occupant to smithereens.

He said as much.

"You've been asked to shift your car and you've refused," Harris told him. "Now we shall have to do it for you."

"Just you try," said Crook. He turned his head, pursed his lips, and the next instant a peal of what sounded like a pig dying in agony split the quiet air.

"Who do you suppose is going to hear that?" inquired Harris contemptuously.

"You'd be surprised," said Crook.

A motorcycle came dashing up the road, turned the corner and joined the group.

"What's going on here?" demanded the policeman riding it.

Harris looked superior and Crook jumped in with the first word.

"I've called to see my ward," he announced. "My name is Crook, I'm a lawyer, as of course you know, and I represent Miss Janice Grey."

"You can represent the Queen of Sheba," exclaimed Harris. "And you're quite as likely to find her here."

"How many prisoners have you got in the cells?" asked Crook interestedly.

"Where on earth did you get the notion that Miss Grey might be here?"

"Inside information. In short, a telephone call from this address."

"Oh, come," said Harris, "someone's been pulling your leg. What on earth's that infernal row?"

For now a new sound could be heard; someone was resolutely thumping on the house knocker.

"Another visitor?" suggested Crook sunnily.

"That'll be my mate," said the police officer. "I mean, that'll be the sergeant."

"What sort of game is this?" Harris exploded. "Who asked . . ." He stared at Crook. "Is this part of your game?"

"Didn't expect to find me in cahoots with the police, did you?" agreed Crook. "Well, I don't mind confessing I'm a bit surprised myself. Still, I've been in queerer company in my time, and—well, a chap in my shoes can't be too particular."

And he returned Harris's red-eyed glare.

The thumping of the knocker ceased. Someone had apparently opened the door. Then Susan came through the side gate of the garden and hesitated on the edge of the group.

"What is it, my dear? This is my daughter," he added to the policeman. "Her husband, Mr. Bates—what was all that noise?"

"There's a policeman asking for you," said Susan.

"That's the one," said Crook. "The one that telephoned me this morning. Said she was Janice Grey. But"—he shook his head—"you don't catch an old bird like me with a pinch of salt."

"What is it?" whispered Susan.

"You should know me," Crook reproved her, and suddenly he went into a lifelike imitation of the voice he'd heard not much more than an hour ago. " 'Mr. Crook? This is Janice Grey. You remember? We met on the train. . . .' How did you know that?"

"I don't know what he's talking about," faltered the girl.

"She must have told you. And your—er—father, did you say?—thought it would be a good idea to get me down here. Much obliged to you, sugar. Gave me the info I needed."

"If anyone had telephoned you from here . . ."

"How else do you think I knew the address? Of course, it was her. Janice Grey couldn't have done it. She didn't know my number, and, bein' forty miles out of London, it wouldn't have been in the local directory. And if you think a girl who's trying to make her getaway is goin' to stop and dial DIR to get my number . . . I had given her a card, it's true, but she left that behind in Paddington, and lucky for her she did. Anyway, if she was flying for her life she'd have dialed 999. There isn't a dame living who doesn't yearn for an opportunity to do that. Then if she'd been cut off, the way you maneuvered it"—he grinned wickedly at Harris—"they'd have sent round to the number she gave to find out what was cooking." His glance wandered to the big gray car. "Sizeable trunk you've got there," he offered—and no one could have guessed how his heart was banging about behind his appalling brown suit—"nearly big enough for a coffin."

Harris laughed shortly. "Help yourself," he said.

Under the watchful eye of the police Crook opened the trunk; there was nothing there that interested him and he let it fall again.

"Well, then, let's take a look-see at the house," he offered. "I brought the dogs of the law with me so everything should be open and aboveboard."

"No doubt you arranged for a search warrant," Harris put in.

"Have you any objection to our coming in, sir?" asked the policeman.

"Because, if you have," cut in Crook, "Robert and me will hold the fort while the sergeant goes back to collect a warrant."

The sergeant looked as though he couldn't make up his mind which of the two he disliked more.

"I suppose," Harris continued smoothly to the officer, "you do realize you're being taken for a ride by this character. Turns up with some fairy tale about a message . . ."

"Oh, I got the message all right," said Crook, "and very grateful to you I am. Might have taken me at least another twenty-four hours to locate you, and, as I've already had occasion to point out—to Miss Plantagenet's sister, to be candid—time is more than money here."

The light was bad and artificial but he could have sworn to a change in that big blank face. Not much of a change but then, if Bill was right and he'd undergone a face lift, his capacity for expression would be severely limited.

"Are we all going to freeze to death standing out here?" demanded the girl in a strained voice.

" 'Three corpses lay on the shining sand'—my point exactly, sugar. I mean, to see that they ain't four. It would save a lot of trouble if you handed the girl over right away. This is one of the games your lot have lost, and you know what they say about a gentleman in defeat."

"Very well," said Harris, "since nothing else will satisfy you . . ."

"Who said anything about being satisfied?" growled Crook.

"I can only hope," Harris went on, paying no attention, "that you chaps have brought a strait jacket with you, because, believe me, you're going to need it."

They filed into the house. In the big bare sitting room Harris opened a box of cigarettes with considerable aplomb and handed them around.

"Don't use 'em myself." he explained.

"Only cigars," amplified Crook.

"Do you mind?" Harris murmured. "I know you don't smoke, Terry—Susan, my dear."

The girl took one nervously. She had made up her face

quite recently and, like most young women nowadays, decided the critical Crook, she'd overdone it. Politely he offered a match.

"No sense offering them to you chaps while you're on duty." Harris nodded to the policemen and put the box away. "Now that we're all here . . ."

"Not all," interrupted the pestilential Crook. "Where's the other fellow?"

"What other fellow?" Harris sounded testy.

"The one who smoked these." Crook indicated a couple of stubs lying in a cut-glass ash tray. "And don't tell me it was your daughter, because there's no thin red line there."

"I've just told you—there's no one else in the house."

"I didn't say he was in the house. I said, where was he?"

"There is no one else."

"Ananias was slain for less," said Crook. "You know who I'm talking about, the chap with a ring. And if you tell me he's still hanging around Waterloo Station waiting for Bill I shan't believe you. And let me assure you"—here his voice dropped to a note so quiet that Bill would have realized they were on the edge of an explosion—"if anything has happened to that girl, you'll all swing." He lifted his big head. "You've got a good-sized property here. Let's have a personally conducted tour, and don't forget the underground passages or the priest's hidey-hole, because I know all the tricks in the pack."

"And probably even have a couple of spare aces up your sleeve," offered Harris. "Well, there's no need for all of us to make the expedition. Susan, you and Terry . . ."

"If two heads are better than one, six must be better than two," said Crook. "And I've taken chances enough in this case as it is."

Harris caught Terry's eye and shrugged. "The chap's mad," that glance said, "but madmen have to be humored."

"After you, sugar," said Crook.

"Don't you give my wife orders," Terry snapped.

"My mother brought me up on a ladies first principle," Crook explained. "And seeing the last shall be first in a better world than this, I'll bring up the rear."

Crook didn't mind taking ordinary chances, but there was no point risking a knife between your shoulders.

"Whoever got me on the phone was pretty well out of breath," Crook recalled. "Let's reverse the usual process and start at the top."

Up the stairs they trudged, a big cumbersome party; Harris in front, then the sergeant, Susan, the other policeman, Bates, as agile as a monkey on a stick, and Crook, stamping up as if he meant to warn every rat on the premises. They passed a number of closed doors, came to the end of the carpeted stairs and made the house ring with their tramp on the naked boards. There were four doors on the top floor, all closed. The sergeant flung them open to reveal what must once have been servants' quarters, gaunt sloping-ceilinged apartments, their ancient furniture still intact, iron bedsteads, yellow wooden dressing tables . . . There were shutters at all the windows.

"We don't use this part of the house," Harris explained.

"I believe you," said Crook heartily. He drew his big finger along a dressertop and brought it back smeared with a kind of oily dust. The window bolts in the first three rooms seemed rusted into their sockets. In the third room luggage was piled —among it an immense-domed black trunk of the sort murderers are supposed to love—but he only gave it a sharp glance and passed on. So they came to the fourth room, and "This is it," said Crook. "This is where she was."

The police looked about them.

"No dust in this attic," Crook pointed out. He laid his hand on the table, then moved toward the bed. Sheets had been folded neatly under the cover. "Thought you didn't use this floor," he suggested. "But someone's been sleeping here quite lately." He walked over to the window. "And these shutters have been opened. They were rusted close in the other rooms." He clanged the bar down and pulled the shutters apart; through the dim panes the untended garden was faintly visible. "Not exactly horticulturists, are you?"

"I tell you, we know nothing about this girl," Harris insisted.

"And the sergeant and me don't believe you."

Terry took a hand. "My wife works up here occasionally. Don't you, Susan?"

"She should apply for a divorce," said Crook, "exiled without a fire, no radio—what work do you do, sugar?" He flung open a cupboard, but there was nothing there.

"I've had enough of this," said Harris. "You can see for yourself, Sergeant, that this girl is not on the premises."

"When d'you expect your friend back?" Crook inquired. "I hope for his own sake he's taking good care of her." But the unaccustomed fear moved in his vitals. He was remembering an occasion years ago when an old woman had died because he'd been too late to save her. Suddenly he slapped his hands together with a reverberation that could almost have been heard in the New Town. "I'm slipping," he exclaimed. "Where do you keep your telephone?"

He was out of the room and pounding down the stairs as he spoke. The others came surging after him.

"What is all this, sir?" the sergeant demanded.

Crook flung open each door as he passed; for all his size and years he went down like a bouncing ball. He had the telephone receiver in his hand before the others caught up with him.

"The operator will be able to tell us if a toll call was put through from here this morning to my office," he explained. He rattled the knob for attracting the operator's attention. "Do they only give you night service here? But no, of course not . . ."

"Put that down," said a voice that made him turn his head sharply.

Harris was standing in the door and in his hand was a small black snub-nosed revolver.

"Here, I say," Crook protested, "you've been seeing too many TV shows."

"No, Mr. Harris," cried Susan desperately. "You can't."

Slowly Crook replaced the receiver. "Now I've heard everything," he declared. "Even in the days of Jane Austen young ladies didn't address their fathers with their surnames. But, of course, she's not your daughter, is she? She's just the wife of one of your accomplices."

"I meant what I said, Mr. Crook."

"I bet you did. You're so deep in this that the shooting of an odd cop or so won't make any difference."

"Terry," said Harris, "go round and get your car and bring it to the front. Then come back here and take over."

"Come with me, Susan," Terry commanded.

"Stay where you are, my dear. Susan will remain here as my hostage," he explained.

"Honor among thieves being a bit rusty in these parts," Crook commented.

"Stay where you are, Bates," the sergeant ordered. "Put that gun down, you can't do yourself any good that way, Mr. Harris. Give it here."

He took a couple of steps forward; instantly the gun barked, and the sergeant reeled. The bullet had struck the floor beside his boot.

"Perhaps that'll convince you I mean business," said Harris in a voice his twin, the man-eating tiger, might have envied. "If I have to fire again the girl will get the first bullet. Now, Terry, do what I say."

There was a second explosion, though this time it wasn't the gun, followed by a spray of glass crashing into the room. A stone fell among them, narrowly missing the police constable. Harris started, his attention momentarily deflected, and in that instant Crook and the policeman jumped. The gun clattered to the floor and the three men went down in a huddle.

Terry caught his wife's arm. "Come on, Susan."

"Not so fast."

Someone else had joined the party, a tall man walking with an almost imperceptible limp. Harris was putting up a terrific fight; Crook dragged himself free and used his feet in a manner that would certainly not have got past the Queensberry Rules. "But when I start working to rule," he observed savagely, "you can run my flag up to half-mast. . . . What the hell are you doing here, Bill?" he added.

Bill Parsons for once seemed to have shed his habitual air of indifference.

"Did you never hear of the seven deadly sins?" he demanded. "And pride's at the top of the list. What made you think you could take on a whole gang single-handed?"

"The police are here," said the sergeant stiffly.

"See what I mean?" said Bill. He looked down at the prostrate and groaning Harris, then stooped closer. "He's had a face-lift all right. Wonder if the police would recognize a picture of him taken, say, three years ago."

"He's going to need another if he don't answer my questions double-quick," Crook promised grimly.

"We'll do the questioning," the sergeant said.

"He'd understand my language better."

Crook looked so threatening that Susan, who by now was on the verge of hysterics, cried, "No, don't. I'll tell you. Oh, Terry, what's the good, they know too much already."

"You know what happens to a squealer," Terry warned her.

"From now on the young lady will have police protection," the sergeant announced.

"Three rousing cheers," said Crook.

"He made me do it," Susan insisted. "He told me to leave the door unlocked, because then she'd be sure to try and escape. Though she was awfully slow, I had to go on fumbling for ages with the shutters before she saw what had happened. Then she locked me in and she ran out—truly she did, Mr. Crook. I saw from the window. She ran through the garden."

"Where no doubt the reception committee was waiting for her. Nice red ring and all."

"I—I didn't see that."

"Too busy ringing me, I suppose. What's his name?"

Susan looked despairingly at her husband, but he had dropped her arm and was staring into space, as though he'd never seen her before and hoped he might never see her again.

"He'd have shot me, Terry," she whispered. "Doesn't that make any difference?"

"That's what you were meant to think," said Crook, as the sergeant snapped the bracelets on Harris's wrists. "But, of course, he wouldn't. Why should he? Once he'd put me and the police down, you could all have taken a powder in your nice fleet of cars. You might even have taken the time off to dig a communal cemetery in the woods." He stopped. "That's where she'll be, of course. How far do the woods extend?"

She shook her head. "I don't know. I've never been there."

Terry made a sudden dive forward for the gun that was still lying where it had dropped from Harris's hand. As his fingers touched it Crook stamped on them smartly, and Bill took possession. The police officer had managed at last to attract the attention of the telephone operator and was issuing orders, like Hitler at the top of his form.

"You've given us a nice bit of cake," Crook told the girl persuasively, "don't hold out on the icing."

But she shook her head in the same desperate way.

"I don't know what they were going to do. They didn't tell me."

"Only used you to bait the trap," agreed Crook, and now he looked scarcely more friendly than Terry had done.

"I had to do what they said," Susan pleaded.

"You try telling that to the judge. It wasn't held a valid excuse at the war trials, and it won't be now."

Her face had seemed so white it didn't appear possible for it to turn any paler, but somehow she managed it.

"That's what Jan said."

This exchange was suddenly interrupted in a dramatic fashion. Everyone heard the sound of a car being driven at a furious pace past the house. Crook and the constable sprang to the window in time to see a small dark vehicle go rushing into the shadows.

Terry laughed and laughed. "Good old Wilf!" he said.

"What's the number of that car?" demanded the sergeant.

"Why not ask Crook, he knows all the answers? And this is one thing my Judas of a wife can't tell you. Figures were never her strong suit."

"No need to trouble the lady," said Bill. "I came that way myself, and it's second nature to me to memorize numbers.

Comes of having learnt so many safe combinations in my youth perhaps."

So he told them the number, and the police got busy on the phone once more.

Fifteen

The car was sighted at Kings Wayland and chased as far as Monkton by two constables on motorcycles. As they made a scissor action to bring it to a halt the driver stamped on the accelerator and took a left-hand curve at about sixty, missing the nearside driver by inches. With an effort the man at the wheel of the car righted her and drove savagely around the curve, but he hadn't allowed for the stationary truck that was unloading there, and it was too late to do anything about it. The car and its driver got considerably the worst of the encounter. While they waited for the ambulance he died without recovering consciousness. They noticed he was wearing a rather striking red ring, and charitably assumed he was a foreigner.

A somewhat macabre feature of the case was that in the trunk of the car was found a neatly wrapped parcel, containing women's clothes, unmarked, anonymous. The carefully printed label was addressed to a refugee organization that was appealing in the national press for unwanted clothes for the homeless. "Don't miss a trick, do they?" observed Crook, when he heard this. "Not much sense disposing of a corpse if said corpse's wardrobe can be traced to you. And there can't be many better ways of getting rid of unwanted effects than packing them off to some organization that'll have 'em unparceled and labeled within the hour."

In the meantime the police were doing a "hunt the thimble" through the orchard and woods behind Hadlington Manor. They had searched the house, basement, garages and sheds without finding a trace of the missing girl. The woods were wild and unproductive, the trees mainly ancient oaks and birches, all rotting from within. During the war some kind of works had been carried on at one end, there were the usual whispers about a ghost, and in fact a skeleton had been discovered there a year or two before. But only the romantically minded believed it was murder. Most likely some old tramp lost his bearings or simply collapsed—medical evidence was to the effect that the victim had been an old man. There had been no attempt to reclaim the woods in the national interest, even during the war when a man practically had to get a license to grow a daisy on his own back lawn. But in connection with the disused works there was a gravel pit overgrown by thorn sprays and long ribbons of weed. No one was sure how deep it was, but deep enough to hide a body till doomsday, if need be.

Crook left the police to dig and delve, and he and Bill did their detecting nearer home.

Crook began to do arithmetic. "Say Susan Baker got on to me the minute the girl was out of earshot. Didn't she say she could see her in the garden? She'd wait to make sure she wasn't coming back maybe, and then get to work. I started out within about five minutes of gettin' the message. Hadlington's about forty miles and the Superb eats up roads like hyenas crunching the bones of dead men. I had to stop at the station to alert the authorities and at the Duck and Daisy—and I could do with a pint of their beer this minute—say, ninety minutes all told."

They were both silent for an instant, thinking what a lot of harm a determined gang could do to a friendless girl in an hour and a half.

"Wilf the Wolf came back while we were in the board room, having our cozy session with Harris and his hardware. He must have come from the woods, Bill. I can't believe he could make that girl go a forty-five-minute walk with him, and he wouldn't leave her there to bear witness against him. What on earth was he doing all that while?"

"Digging a grave, perhaps," said Bill, "and I don't mean his own."

Crook's hand caught him with a grip like a lobster's claw.

"Bill, remember that shed full of gardening gear. Well, was there a spade there? Can you remember?"

They beetled back and Bill played his powerful flashlight over the moldy floor. There was an immense fork, with mud as hard as stone on its crooked tines; there was a hoe, a rake, a pair of rusty shears and a trowel that would come in very handy for putting in herbaceous plants, "but no sexton would thank you for the loan of that," as Crook said, "and that's just what Wilf is—an amateur sexton."

Almost hand in hand, the long and the short of it, like a modern version of the babes in the wood, they went hastening down the path.

The police had brought a walkie-talkie and they could hear voices echoing eerily among the trees. By now the light had faded from the sky, and darkness was spreading like a blanket. Crook stared upward as if he thought the heavens would be split asunder and a Christmas-card angel, blowing a long thin trumpet, would emerge to point them the way.

"There's still something screwy," Crook murmured. "Why did he leave the spade? That's the sort of thing people notice. And don't tell me he took it away in the car. It's in the woods somewhere, waiting to fill in the grave."

"He could have left her quite near the entrance to the woods," speculated Bill, "and come back to get help. She may only have been a small girl, but it's always a surprise to the amateur how heavy a corpse can be."

"They're a right crowd, aren't they?" he observed grimly. "Every man for himself, none of the old Eton-and-Harrow spirit about them. Hullo, what gives?"

From the direction where the police lights were bobbing among the trees an excited clamor arose. Crook cupped his hands around his mouth and yelled. "Tally-ho!" he bawled.

A voice came back. "That you, Mr. Crook? This way."

They came crashing through the undergrowth, tripping

over hidden holes, tangling themselves in the briars that spread in every direction. The police were standing in a clump, staring not at the girl but at a newly dug pit; a pile of earth was erected like a wall against some tree trunks; and a spade, freshly smeared with the clods, lay on the ground.

"The valley of dying men," muttered Crook, hunching his big shoulders in a gesture that in anyone else would have been a shudder. Everything here spoke of death and desolation. There was even a theatrical rook that expressed itself with an improbable caw and flew out of the leafless boughs where last year's great black untidy nests hung like tumors against that lowering sky. Even a wandering hyena, thought Crook, might have legged it for some more cheerful spot.

One of the policemen said, "She must be a big girl; you could bury twin sergeants there." And Crook cried out, "That's it, of course; why Wilf came back to the house instead of staying on and finishing the job. This was going to be a communal grave. 'And in death they were not divided,' and what my guardian angel 'ud say when the graves were opened and I was found with a pretty young woman—though I daresay she wouldn't look so pretty then—is anyone's guess."

He felt Bill's hand on his arm and shut up abruptly. Years ago as a boy of seventeen Parsons had been buried for a time in a collapsed trench in France, and though he never spoke of it he never altogether forgot it either. And tonight the darkness and the gaping hole and the sheer inhumanity of the situation shook him up worse than he'd been shaken for years.

"It puzzled me all along why they didn't finish the job," Crook went on, after a moment. "Of course, they were out to get both their birds with one stone. Well, I ask you. How many people come through these woods in a twelvemonth, particularly at this time of the year? The brambles could have grown waist-high before anyone found that grave, and by that time it could have been Hitler and his girl friend under the nettles."

"I wonder how they meant to explain the car away," Bill speculated.

"We ain't too far from the coast, traveling due east from Hadlington, and there'd not be much traffic on the roads at night. A car can crash over a lonely bit of headland, and if the driver ain't found, well, we know the date fixed for the sea yielding up the dead that are in it, and that's Judgment Day. Leave one of the doors open and the tides might sweep a body out to sea." He heaved a sigh that nearly blew one of the disused nests out of the treetops.

"She won't be far from here," declared the sergeant, and they all moved in, their feet rustling in a depth of leaves that wouldn't have shamed a prize Aubusson carpet.

They found her propped upright in a clump of trees whose tatterdemalion trunks leaned together to form a natural tent. If you hadn't been looking for her you could have passed her half a dozen times without a suspicion. She must, before collapsing into unconsciousness, have recognized her peril, for she had struggled hard for her life; there were scratches on wrists and hands, and the constable's lantern showed a blue bruise under one eye. Her clothes were disordered and her stockings torn to ribbons. Somewhere, flying from her persecutor, she had lost a shoe.

"Just as well young Frank is under lock and key," remarked Crook grimly. "If Wilf knows his onions he'll take a quiet nosedive into the nearest river." (They didn't know at that stage that this was approximately what he had done.) "It's like that rhyme," Crook went on.

"I found my dear little doll, dears,
As I roamed through the woods one day.
You could pass her a couple of yards, dears,
And never perceive where she lay.
One arm trodden off by the cows, dears,
And her hair not the least bit curled,
But for old times' sake she is still, dears,
The prettiest doll in the world."

There wasn't much prettiness about her now; blood had dried in the sharp wind over a cut on the ashen face, and there was a second bruise coming up on her jaw that might have been caused by a fall, but in Crook's opinion was more likely to be due to a fist.

One of the younger constables spoke. "Is she dead, sir?"

"Of course she's not dead," snapped Crook. "My clients don't pass out so easy. She's got everything to live for, and this case has kept the undertakers busy enough as it is. And"—he was peeling off his brown coat as he spoke—"though it's cold enough to freeze a brass monkey, a healthy young woman don't die of exposure in a couple of hours. Someone's had an interest in this abomination of desolation at one time," he added thoughtfully. "This"—and he indicated the rents in her dress—"was done by barbed wire."

"She's been drugged all right," said Bill, who was a bit of a Jack-of-all-trades. "Probably the needle unless she had something to drink before she got away." He took a flask of brandy out of his hip pocket.

"Macintosh, you get along to the house and tell them to bring that stretcher double-quick," the sergeant ordered. "And the same goes for an ambulance. And I don't care if it's reserved for the Queen of Sheba, for once she can stand down."

"That's the boy," agreed Crook, feeling more affection for the police than he'd done in years.

For all his vaunted optimism, his heart was beating painfully. Tick-tock, tick-tock, it seemed to him as loud as Big Ben. And he felt—and said—he could have made a stretcher in the time it took the chaps to bring one. But they had to wait. There wasn't a convenient hurdle or the door of a shed they could utilize, all they could do was try and keep her warm, massaging the icy hands and feet.

Crook went in the ambulance to the hospital, *in loco parentis,* he said, and Bill, leaving his own car for one of the constables to drive back, operated the Superb.

It was obvious from the matron's manner that Crook was not, and never would be, her favorite man.

"We'll let you know how Miss Grey progresses," she said.

"O.K." Crook beamed. "You'll find me in the corridor."

"Out of the question," snapped the matron.

"Then I'll flop down in the Superb. Look, she'll want to

see one human face when she does come round, and me, I can sleep anywhere. Having got this far, I'm not risking any wicked-fairy stuff where my girl's concerned."

Of course, he reflected, the face she'd want to see was young Frank, but she'd be able to walk to London before they'd unwound the red tape that was binding him.

Matron put on a lot of dog about the hospital's responsibility, but Crook retorted that Jan was his responsibility, though he was prepared, in the circumstances, to delegate some of it in the right quarter. Matron went nearly black in the face, but she might as well have saved her breath. She'd find it easier to move the Rock of Gibraltar—well, no harder, anyway—than dislodge Crook once his mind was made up.

"This girl is my ward," insisted Crook, as though in capital letters.

She even appealed to the police, but they were playing safe. They said Crook would at least be a barrier between her nurses and the press, who might be expected at any moment. It was while he was waiting that Crook got the news about Wilf; he was past giving verbal evidence, but the condition of his clothes, the thorns, the mud, the dead leaves in the car, all spoke for him. And, in addition, there were the footprints in the earth piled around that unhallowed grave.

Crook, who didn't mind how often a thing had been said if it met the case, observed that nothing so became the dead man's life as his leaving of it.

"Jam for Harris," he remarked to Bill some time later. "Like a bet that he'll cheat the gallows even now? You'll see, he'll have an alibi for the night Routh was killed, and though the whole party's held responsible for the fatal blow, if you can prove you weren't even there, even though you were the mind behind the machine—well, a nice crooked lawyer like Penrose could probably swing it. Then there are the girls—well, ours isn't dead and she ain't going to die."

"What about the one who did?" inquired Bill.

"We know No. 8 Spring Terrace wasn't exactly an exclusive residence. The window cleaner will be persuaded to tell his story about the red ring, and even if the jury have the sense to discredit most of his yarn, there'll be that faint residue of doubt. It would be different if Frank could swear to the identity of the chap he saw leaving the house. He knows it was Harris and so do I, but knowing ain't proof. And the chap who disposed of Pat Wylie wore a ring, which Harris don't, and that one's answering graver charges in another world. One way and another, I'd say our Mr. H. has got things sewn up very neat."

"And the British taxpayer is expected to give three rousing cheers at the prospect of keeping him for the next twenty years or so. Even our benevolent British justice isn't likely to let him out in a hurry. And, of course, there's Terry Bates."

"You could say he comes out of this better than any of them," said Crook. "He's refused to squeal on Harris, and, seeing we've no third degree in this country, the odds are he'll go on keeping his mouth shut. The girl will be able to plead that she was acting under her husband's orders, which is no doubt true, and she had no part in any of the murders or attempted murders. Jan says she treated her as kindly as she could in the circumstances, and she gave the police the wigwag at a crucial moment. Not that Terry will ever forgive her, but then she'll have time to forget what he looks like before he's returned to the common herd."

With the police to back him, Crook had got Frank James released in record time; when the young man emerged from the prison he found the Superb waiting at the gate.

"Hop in," invited Crook, leaning back to open the door.

"Where's Jan?" demanded Frank.

"I said hop in. Well, she's waited long enough, hasn't she?"

Frank got in. Jan was there, of course. Crook didn't ask them where they wanted to go, he knew it would be a waste of breath. The marriage-license office wasn't open at this hour, so he drove to a house in Paddington.

Miss Hiscock met them on the step. "Well," she said characteristically, "you've got yourself in a nice mess, haven't you, going off with strange men. It's about time you settled down."

"I suppose my room isn't free," said Jan in a dreamy voice.

"Who do you think wants it now, with my last two lodgers being taken off by the police?" demanded Emma Hiscock. It wasn't an altogether accurate statement, but Crook didn't correct her.

"Oh, come on," he urged, taking Emma by the arm, "they won't remember we're born till the time comes to send round the bits of wedding cake. And it's no sense reminding them at this stage that if it hadn't been for you we might be having the funeral march instead of the wedding ditto."

He guided her along to the kitchen, that glowed comfortably, and he hauled a bottle of something equally comforting out of his pocket.

"Get the glasses, sugar," he said.

About the Author

ANTHONY GILBERT is the pseudonym for an English author who writes novels of contemporaneous English life and probably does not wish to confuse the authorship of those books with his murder mysteries. The name Anthony Gilbert has become synonymous with that of Mr. Crook, insouciant criminal lawyer, who has appeared as the *deus ex machina* in these tales of violence.

612